Three Months Pregnant.

"You *are* going to keep the baby," Heath said.

Her eyes widened. "How dare you? How dare you believe I'd do anything else?"

Too late Heath remembered that Amy had highly romantic views of family. No babies out of wedlock. White, splashy weddings. Of course she'd keep the baby.

Oh hell, she was about to cry again. Heath moved closer.

"No!" she said.

"I can understand why you're angry with me, Amy."

"Can you?" She turned her head away and pursed the pink rosebud mouth that had been the subject of his most recent fantasies. "Take me back to work, to Saxon's Folly."

He narrowed his gaze, taking in the rebellious glitter in her golden eyes. "You're not going back to work. I won't allow it."

The glitter intensified. "You can't stop me."

"Of course I can."

Dear Reader,

When I was twelve years old, I visited Groot Constantia. It's the home of Simon van der Stel, first Governor of the Cape of Good Hope in 1691, and the man who had the foresight to realize that grapes would be perfect for the region and established vast tracks of vineyards around the house.

The estate is glorious. The Cape Dutch house has a timeless presence. But what roused my interest more than anything else was the identity of the mysterious Constance for whom the estate is named. One story says that Simon van der Stel built the house for his beloved, Constance, that her statue is set into the front gable of the house, but that she died before she could appreciate his labor of love. Another tale speculates that Constance was his lover and inspired the Vin de Constance that was wildly popular later in nineteenth-century Europe— Napoleon is rumored to have had it shipped to St. Helena in his final years of life.

That visit to Groot Constantia started my love affair with vineyards—especially those steeped in history and romance. So when I first discussed THE SAXON BRIDES miniseries with my editor and she loved the idea of a vineyard setting…I was utterly thrilled. I'd recently spent some time in New Zealand's Hawkes Bay—a wine-making region that I find very beautiful, historic and incredibly romantic—and so Saxon's Folly came to life.

I hope you enjoy Amy and Heath's story…I had a wonderful time creating it.

Take care,

Tessa

PREGNANCY PROPOSAL

TESSA RADLEY

Published by Silhouette Books
America's Publisher of Contemporary Romance

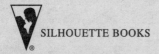

SILHOUETTE BOOKS

ISBN-13: 978-0-373-76914-8
ISBN-10:   0-373-76914-8

Recycling programs
for this product may
not exist in your area.

PREGNANCY PROPOSAL

Visit Silhouette Books at www.eHarlequin.com

Printed in U.S.A.

TESSA RADLEY

loves traveling, reading and watching the world around her. As a teen, Tessa wanted to be an intrepid foreign correspondent. But after completing a Bachelor of Arts degree and marrying her sweetheart, she became fascinated by law and ended up studying further and practicing as an attorney in a city practice.

A six-month break traveling through Australia with her family reawoke the yen to write. And life as a writer suits her perfectly; traveling and reading count as research, and as for analyzing the world...well, she can think "what if" all day long. When she's not reading, traveling or thinking about writing, she's spending time with her husband, her two sons or her zany and wonderful friends. You can contact Tessa through her Web site, www.tessaradley.com.

To all my readers—this story is for each one of you.
Every time I receive a note telling me how much
you've enjoyed one of my books, you make my day!

One

Heath Saxon's footsteps echoed against the polished stone floor as he walked through the deserted reception area of Saxon's Folly Estate and Wines. He had expected more fanfare over his return as winemaker to the illustrious Saxon's Folly winery, located in the Hawkes Bay on the east coast of New Zealand. An olive branch from his father on his first morning would have been welcome. A fatted calf even better. After all, it wasn't every day that the family bad boy came back.

So maybe he hadn't come a long way in miles—he lived over in the next valley and most Thursday nights came for dinner—but the emotional gap he'd covered by returning spanned more than physical distance. Ever since that final, fierce altercation with his father he'd stayed well away from the winery itself where he'd once toiled long hours creating fine wines using a blend of science and art. Business and family just didn't mix.

Now he stared around the winery. The oak vats smelled

exactly as he remembered from when he'd been chief wine-maker here.

"Heath…"

Every muscle tightened at the sound of the soft voice behind him. *Amy.* He turned and his eyes drank in the sight of her.

A tentative smile played on her pearly-pink lips. Her bobbed dark-chocolate hair was smoothly tucked behind her ears, gold studs glinting in her lobes. Subtle makeup, only enough to hide the dark circles beneath her golden eyes, nothing more. If it hadn't been for those molten eyes, she would've looked like a schoolgirl. Not frumpy, but almost too neat to be true in the white shirt with a rounded collar and the navy skirt.

Innocent.

Or maybe not. Inside he sighed silently. He'd planned to avoid Amy today. All week. Forever, if he could. He started to move away. "Yes, Amy?"

The smile faded. "Taine just called in sick. He says it's a only a sore throat and he should be back at work tomorrow."

Taine was one of the Saxon's Folly cellar hands. "That's fine."

"He says to give him a call and he'll give you an update on what he was supposed to do today."

"I'll call him back."

Amy hovered. "Thanks, Heath."

"My pleasure." He bit off dark thoughts about what really was his pleasure. Amy's mouth swollen with his kisses…Amy lying on his bed…Amy saying—

Hell, why was he torturing himself like this?

He need look no further than her pursed pale-pink mouth to know that none of that was going to happen.

"Heath?"

"Yes?" He'd tried to control his frustration but Amy's amber-gold eyes darkened at his tone. "Sorry, I was thinking about finding Jim—" the other cellar hand "—to let him know Taine wouldn't be in."

"I simply wanted to be the first to say welcome back." Pursing her mouth into a tight bud, she tipped her nose in the air and turned on her heel and stalked away.

Heath was left watching her trim bottom in the demure navy skirt, her straight back retreat. He restrained the fierce urge to swear.

First day back and he'd managed to offend Amy Wright.

Just great.

So what else was new? He should be used to it by now. Ever since he'd waded in and bought the bankrupt Chosen Valley vineyard from Ralph Wright, Amy's father, he'd been separated from her and his family by more than just the range of hills between the two wineries that was appropriately named The Divide.

His heroic gesture had offended even Amy, who hadn't recognized it for what it was—an attempt to rescue her and her father from a crippling cycle of debt. As for his own father, Phillip Saxon had seen it as an attempt to go into direct competition with Saxon's Folly. Heath shook his head. Perhaps his armour was so tarnished no one could recognize his good intentions any more. So he'd retreated into grim silence, and the gap between him and his family—and him and Amy— had widened.

And now he was back at Saxon's Folly. Because Saxon's Folly needed a chief winemaker. Caitlyn Ross, the previous winemaker, had left to get married—to start a new life in Spain with Rafaelo, the half brother Heath had slowly grown to like and respect over the past few weeks.

Of course his father hadn't asked him to return. The old man was too full of stiff-necked pride for that. It had been Caitlyn who'd begged him to come back so that she could leave Saxon's Folly with a clear conscience.

It felt strange to be back. Heath's gaze narrowed as Amy disappeared through the arch that led into the reception area.

Heath suspected that once again his soft heart was going to cost him. Dearly.

For Amy the morning passed in a rush. The phone hadn't stopped ringing and everyone demanded her attention. With Saxon's Folly Summer Festival—a Christmas Eve celebration of the ripening grapes—now a little over three weeks away, a final panic had settled in.

"Amy could you order more candles for the carols ceremony?"

"Amy, would you mind getting these brochures printed?"

"Don't forget to hire three marquees for the festival, Amy."

"Omigod, Amy! Kelly Christie just called to say that she'd like to cover the festival for the Christmas Day edition of her midday TV show."

Most of the organizing was already done—with some things, like booking the jazz bands, done a year in advance—but last-minute crazy details like Kelly Christie kept cropping up. It hadn't been this bad last year. Amy wasn't stupid; she was the reason why there had been a constant stream of people arriving at her desk with requests. It had been going on—albeit on a slightly less insane scale—for weeks. No, make that months. Two months to be precise.

The Saxons were worried about her. She wished she could tell them that she was fine but they didn't ask. Their concern just lay in their eyes, in the way they hovered around her, coming with requests in person rather than phoning or e-mailing what they wanted through to her.

The only one who didn't have a million questions to ask or a zillion mundane tasks to keep her busy today was Heath Saxon.

Black sheep. Hothead. Bad boy.

She shut her eyes. She should've been grateful that he'd

kept his distance on his first day back, she should be saying thanks to—

"Amy, do you know where Alyssa is?"

Eyes snapping open, she found Megan, the youngest Saxon, in front of her.

Megan was staring at her in a way that made Amy's heart sink.

"Are you all right, sweetie?"

"I'm fine," Amy reassured her. For the past two months everyone had been handling her with kid gloves. It was time for the PA of Saxon's Folly to get back to normal. "Sorry, you caught me daydreaming. I think Alyssa went into town with your brother."

"With Joshua?"

Naturally Alyssa had gone with Joshua, her fiancé. Who else could she have gone with? Heath, of course, he was back at Saxon's Folly. But then Amy got a good look at Megan's face. She looked sad. Megan must be thinking about Roland. Amy swallowed and glanced away before the tears came.

There was a silence.

"Sweetie, don't be so hard on yourself. Give yourself a break." The gentleness in Megan's voice made Amy's throat grow thick.

She bit back the sob that threatened. "Really, I'm fine!"

But Megan's concerned eyes told her she didn't believe it.

"Okay, I'm just feeling a little emotional today." Amy dragged in a shaky breath. She pushed the strand of hair that had fallen over her forehead back behind her ears. "An Auckland florist called. Roland ordered a bouquet for me… they wanted to know what colours I was choosing for the wedding, so they could select suitable ribbons for the bouquet."

"Oh, my God." Megan covered her mouth. "Sweetie, I'm so sorry." She came forward in a rush.

Bracing her hands on the counter separating them, Amy shrank away. If Megan hugged her she was going to cry. She knew it. She shook her head frantically. "It's okay, really it is."

"No, it's not okay. Roland——"

"—is dead." She didn't want more pity. "And there won't be a wedding." Megan must be hurting too. Roland had been her adopted brother, though no one had known he was adopted until a little over a month ago.

"Amy, I'm so sorry." Megan covered Amy's hands where they lay on top of the reception counter.

Amy fisted her fingers. "Me too. He wasn't supposed to die."

"No, you were supposed to get married…live happily ever after. That's all you—everyone—ever wanted."

Amy's mouth trembled. "I think I was fourteen when I decided I was going to marry Roland Saxon. I told him when I turned sixteen but he said I was too young for him. So I proposed at my seventeenth birthday dinner." After he'd kissed her outside in the romance of the dark summer's night…kisses meant true love and marriage, didn't they?

How young she'd been. How very idealistic.

Megan's cell phone rang.

"You'd better get that," Amy said, sliding a hand out from under Megan's to rip a tissue from the box on her desk and determinedly wipe her eyes. The outside line rang, so she picked it up and said in a bright voice, "Saxon's Folly Estate and Wines," and then started to note down a booking for a tour group that wanted to do a wine tasting.

Megan's call ended. Clearly she wanted to talk. But Amy didn't. She gave Megan a quick smile, before huddling down behind the counter and starting to describe the various packages available for tour groups. When the call ended she looked up.

To her relief Megan had gone.

"I'm worried about Amy."

Heath stilled in the act of counting wine bottles shelved in order of vintage in the wine-master's cellar. A bottle of every wine the winery had produced since it was started by Spanish monks almost a century ago was stored there. At the sound of Megan's voice he stared fixedly at the cursive gold print on the label of the bottle in front of him.

Finally Heath turned his head and met his sister's direct gaze. "We're all concerned."

"Roland's death has been hard on all of us." Megan gave a sniff, belying her composure.

"At least we've got each other to share the grief with," Heath said. "You, me and Joshua have always been close."

"Exactly! But Amy's so alone, it breaks my heart. She pretends she's fine. But she's so fragile," said Megan, coming in and closing the door behind her. "I'm sure she's lost more weight."

Heath shrugged helplessly. "Dad suggested she take time off. Joshua suggested it. I suggested it. She took two weeks and came back looking worse than she had before. I don't know what to do next."

Megan leant against the antique desk where every chief winemaker at Saxon's Folly had worked, and said, "The wedding would have taken place in two weeks. She must be thinking about it all the time."

"Probably." Heath could feel himself growing tense. He'd spent so long refusing to think of Amy's forthcoming marriage to his brother that he hated being reminded of the occasion. Though he was certain Amy had thought of little but the frothy romantic event. Beneath that goody-two-shoes exterior lurked the heart of a romantic.

"She needs to be kept busy."

"Why?" He stared at his sister. In his opinion, Amy needed a break, a rest, time to reflect. Time to grieve.

"So that she doesn't get a chance to think about Roland's death." His younger sister loved organizing other people. "I'm going to get her even more involved in helping with the festival." Megan gave a shudder. "She was in the car with him—the memories must give her nightmares."

Heath closed his mind against the night his brother had died. He didn't want to remember…

Instead, he pondered his sister's suggestion. The annual Saxon's Folly Summer Festival took place the day before Christmas, a busy time of year. And it took a lot of work to make it happen. In the past Roland and Megan had done most of the organizing. Roland had been marketing manager and had worked closely with Megan, whose main role was PR. Since Roland's death Megan had been assuming more of the marketing role—and she'd drawn in Alyssa Blake, Joshua's fiancée, to do some of the overflow PR work. For all he knew, Amy might enjoy being more involved, too.

"That's not a bad idea," he said finally, "but the festival isn't going to replace her wedding."

Megan rocked back on her hands against the desk and rolled her eyes to the ceiling. "I know that, Heath."

"She has to face the fact that Roland is gone." Heath turned back to the wall and pulled a random bottle out of its pigeonhole.

"She knows he's gone." His sister sounded impatient. "That's why she's so lost."

Heath wasn't so sure. Amy had retreated into a place where no one could reach her. She'd frozen everyone out. He was almost certain it was her way of escaping reality.

Of hiding from the truth…

He stared unseeingly at the bottle in his hands. When she came out from that place, there was going to be a lot of pain: she was going to have to accept that Roland was gone. Forever. And at some point Amy was going to have to realise that she was still young, that her life wasn't over. That she still had a chance to live…and love.

"Maybe you can talk to her, Heath." Megan's voice held the forceful determination that he knew all too well.

No. He didn't want to talk to Amy—and he doubted she'd listen. He'd done enough harm already.

He slotted the bottle of wine back into its pigeonhole and walked over to the desk Megan leaned against, dropping down into the antique leather chair behind it and propping his elbows on the blotter.

"No." His answer was very final.

Megan swivelled around and eyed him curiously. "Did you two have a fight?"

"A fight?" He frowned at his sister. "What do you take me for? I couldn't do that to Amy. Not at this time."

"I thought it might be your idea of shock therapy."

"Shock therapy?" *God.* Heath raked his hands through his hair. "No way." Maybe he'd had some misguided intentions. But not shock therapy. Nothing that deliberate—or cold-blooded.

"Okay, I got it wrong." Megan picked up the exclusive catalogue of wines that they mailed to Saxon's Folly's top customers and flipped idly through it, her bangs falling forward over her eyes. "I noticed you've been avoiding her for the past couple of weeks and wondered. I thought you two were friends."

Heath was relived to be out of his sister's sharp eyesight. Since Roland's funeral Amy had rebuffed every attempt he'd made to offer comfort. Finally, he'd given up and taken to avoiding her.

"Not really." Not since she'd turned sixteen. What he felt for Amy wasn't friendship; it was a whole lot more dangerous.

"But surely after what you did for her—"

"What did I do for her?" he said too quickly.

The catalogue landed on the desk with a thud. "You bought the vineyard after Ralph ran it into the ground."

"I didn't do that for Amy." Heath folded his arms across his chest. "Whatever gave you that idea? I did it for myself. Once it became clear that Saxon's Folly wasn't big enough for me and Dad I had two choices—go work for someone else, or set up my own show."

"But why Chosen Valley? Surely you realised that buying a vineyard that close would get into Dad's face?"

"It was a good choice." He didn't elaborate further. He didn't need to—he'd been proved right.

"You didn't have to pay what you did—"

"It was a fair market price."

"But you could've—"

"Give it a rest, Megan."

"And you arranged a job for Amy here at Saxon's Folly."

He shrugged. "So what? I arranged for Dad to employ Caitlyn, too." He grinned at his sister, intent on distracting her, and took refuge in humour that he didn't feel. "Maybe I have frustrated latent urges to be a hotshot corporate recruiter."

Megan burst out laughing. "You? A hotshot recruiter? Never. You're a softie. Your only latent urges are to help people. You arranged that job for Amy because you felt sorry for her, because after being brought up as Daddy's princess she didn't have a whole lot of marketable skills and you—"

Relieved that Megan thought his latent urges had been motivated by altruism rather than something far more basic, Heath growled, "Back off!"

His sister gave him a triumphant look. "I will for now."

But once she'd gone, Heath brooded. If Megan had noticed that he was avoiding Amy, others would, too, and the last thing he needed was questions. The sooner he made his peace with Amy the better.

Amy saw him coming.

She ducked her head down and busied herself with entering a column of sales figures into the computer. When Heath finally stopped in front of the counter she gave a fake little start and her hands fluttered to her breast. "Oh, Heath, you surprised me."

She got the feeling that her deception hadn't worked. Colour rose to her cheeks. Amy never lied. Discomforted at being caught in the act, her hands stilled on her shirtfront, a barrier from behind which she could watch Heath.

He was tall, his hair so dark in comparison to Roland's bright-red mane. Heath's eyes were black. Brooding. Unreadable. The darkness underlined by the black T-shirts and black jeans he normally wore.

Black Saxon.

As a youngster he'd gotten into a lot of fights and gained a terrible reputation. She could remember a period when Heath had always seemed to have his eyes blackened, which was when the Black Saxon nickname had stuck. But he'd always been kind to her.

He'd been a rebel. He'd fought with his father, resisting his authority. His parents had been only too pleased to pack him off to university. She'd heard tales of hazings and wild parties, but when he'd returned he'd changed. Matured. For a while she'd considered him one of her best friends.

But somewhere along the line it had changed. He'd withdrawn. The silences between them had become uncomfortable. And when her father had almost lost the winery, Heath had charged in and bought it—no doubt for a song. Though he'd felt guilty enough to arrange a job for her at the winery. It had suited her…and brought her closer to Roland.

After the night Roland died, she and Heath no longer seemed to know what to say to each other.

She didn't even know what he thought about the discovery that Roland was adopted…or how he felt about the arrival of his half brother last month. Or what he thought about Caitlyn leaving.

But then she'd been so caught up in her own woes she

hadn't asked. Her self-absorption made her shudder with embarrassment. She needed to remedy that. "Do you think Caitlyn will be happy with Rafaelo?"

He gave her a strange look. "Why shouldn't she be?"

"I thought—" Amy broke off, flushing.

He came closer. "You thought what?"

"Uh…I thought that you and Caitlyn had something going."

He threw his head back and laughed out loud. "Me and Caitlyn?"

Despite the flash of white teeth from this close, Amy could see his black-devil's eyes weren't laughing. "I thought…"

"You thought what?" There was a fixed intensity in his eyes, an intensity that made her want to shudder in discomfort again.

"She came back from university with you." Amy glanced away from that penetrating gaze and fiddled with the computer keys, opening a file, feeling foolish.

She wasn't clever—not like Caitlyn Ross whom everybody knew was supersmart. Caitlyn had gone to university on a science scholarship. By contrast, Amy had tried hard at school, done exactly as she was told, but though she'd usually gotten a prize at the end of the year it was always for effort or citizenship rather than academic brilliance. *Teacher's pet.* The unkind taunt of her schoolmates came back in an unwelcome blast.

She felt, rather than saw, Heath shrug. "I tutored Caitlyn. It was no secret that she was going to go places. So I told Dad about her, and for once Dad actually listened to what I had to say." A bitter slant distorted his sculpted mouth. "He offered her a vacation job. She was so good there was no way he was going to let her go."

"Did it hurt that your father became her mentor? That she took your job as chief winemaker?" Amy had wondered about that when he bought Chosen Valley.

"Nah, when I resigned I suggested Dad promote her."

"So he took your advice again." Maybe Heath didn't see how much stock Phillip Saxon placed in him. It wouldn't hurt to point it out. It was awful that there was such a rift between the two Saxon men.

"He would've been stupid not to have."

Amy gave him a quick upward glance. "Maybe it was because you've always held her in such high regard that I thought you'd end up married."

Heath's shoulders rose under the close-fitting black T-shirt, then dropped nonchalantly.

He certainly didn't look heartbroken. A frown wrinkled Amy's forehead. She'd been so certain that Caitlyn had wanted Heath. She'd caught Caitlyn watching him in the past, a soft, yearning look on her face. All that had changed with the Spaniard's arrival. Rafaelo had swept her off her feet. Emotion clogged up her throat. "Oh, well, I hope Caitlyn and Rafaelo will be happy together. Have they set a wedding date yet?"

Heath gave her a sharp glance. "Next year, I believe."

A wedding…

Amy bit her lip and looked down at the keyboard. Her lip began to hurt. She bit harder.

"Amy?"

She didn't look up. She hit the keyboard with a series of random taps. A tear splashed onto the spacebar.

"Amy!"

She bent her head lower. Heath mustn't see her crying. Not him, of all people.

Too late. He'd come around the counter. He was standing beside her; she could hear his breathing, loud in the private space behind the counter. Amy's shoulders started to shake. Inside she felt hot and tight as if she were going to burst. As if she could no longer hold it all in—all the grief and emotion she'd been pressing down, terrified it might explode out.

"Hush."

Heath's hands came down on her shoulders. She stiffened. But the thickness in her throat grew more painful. She swallowed. That hurt. She could barely breathe.

He pulled. The typist's chair spun round. She caught one glimpse of his face, saw the torment in his dark eyes, and hurriedly shut her own eyes as tightly as she could. But still the tears leaked out, burning down her cheeks.

There was a rustle of fabric, as if he was crouching down. But she didn't dare open her eyes. Then Heath's hands tightened on her shoulders, pulling her from the chair. She gasped as she slid. Suddenly he was no longer behind her, and she landed in a sprawl across his thighs where he knelt beside the chair, the slim-fitting navy skirt riding up to expose bare pale thigh.

She tried desperately to tug it down.

The linen resisted. A moment later Heath's arms closed around her, drawing her tightly against his chest. He smelt warm and male, of sun and dust and a hint of lemon. She made a little choking sound and buried her face against his shirtfront.

"I know you loved him for so long. I know there's a huge hole in your life now."

The choke became a sob.

Her throat was hot. Her insides twisted. She wanted to order Heath to be quiet, to release her, to go away, but she couldn't find the strength.

Tears rushed down her cheeks.

"Cry all you want, Amy. Let it all out."

She couldn't bear for him to see her like this, in such a state. He was so contained, so controlled. He was no longer the impulsive bad boy; he'd grown up. Whereas she'd regressed. She'd gone from being the good girl who did everything right every time to someone she didn't know. Someone who felt like she'd lost total control of herself, her life.

Darn it, she didn't even know why she was crying. The tears

had come out of nowhere. For a moment she allowed her body to sag and great gasps of pain escaped her. Heath didn't move, didn't speak. He just kept her close in the circle of his arms. Embarrassed, Amy gave a gulp and summoned all her strength.

She pulled away from him. A horrified glance revealed that there were unsightly damp patches over the front of Heath's immaculate black T-shirt where she'd blubbered like a baby.

Kneeling on the carpet, she reached for a tissue from the box on the desk. No way was she dabbing at the sodden patches on his shirt with a tissue. She wasn't going near him. Sniffling, she retreated further and said, "I'm so sorry. I don't know what's wrong with me. I can't seem to stop crying."

He reached for her. "You've had a terrible time and I haven't helped—"

She fought her way out his arms and leapt to her feet, cannoning into the chair and causing it to shoot sideways. All at once the room started to tip sideways, before righting and tipping back the other way.

This must be what an earthquake felt like. Her vision turned spotty. "Heath, I don't feel well."

Her legs crumpled beneath her. She glimpsed a foggy Heath lurching toward her.

Everything went dark.

Two

To Amy's dismay, Heath high-handedly packed her into his flashy silver Lamborghini, drove her to his home—*her* birthplace, the home where *she'd* grown up—and summoned a doctor.

He'd hurried her past his concerned housekeeper, through the entrance hall and up the staircase to the guest bedroom on the first floor. When she'd last seen this room it had been a faded sky-blue, in desperate need of refurbishment. Heath had done that. The dove's-egg blue and ivory striped wallpaper was fresh and elegant, the padded bedcover pristine, and two paintings in hues of blues and greens hung over the queen-sized bed. Once he was satisfied that she was comfortable, Heath crossed to the window, pushed the heavy ivory drapes fully open and released the sash window to let in fresh, country air.

She waited for him to turn, then lifted her chin, saying brightly, "I'm fine now. I don't need a doctor." Amy knew she must sound like a chirpy little sparrow. But there was nothing wrong with her. She knew it. Now if only she could make Heath understand that too. Except he wasn't listening.

He was grey under his tan. His lips were set in a tight line and his eyes held a determined look that warned her that she wasn't going to change his mind.

"I called Dr. Shortt during your faint. He should be here soon."

"Dr. Shortt? But I haven't seen him for years. Not since I last had chicken pox." That had been the tenth anniversary of her mother's death and her father had been in a state. Amy had been fifteen, too old to be contracting chicken pox and definitely too old to be receiving house calls—in her teenaged opinion.

"Who is your doctor now? I'll call them if you don't want Dr. Shortt—though he's dropped everything to come see you."

"I haven't been to the doctor in years. I'm as healthy as a horse." Amy was still arguing five minutes later when Dr. Shortt entered the room, a worn black bag clutched under his arm. Except for a few extra pounds around his middle and a little more grey hair above his ears, the doctor hadn't changed from the last time she'd seen him.

"Amy, my girl, what have we done to ourselves?"

And he still spoke to her as if she were a child. Amy glared at Heath, unfairly blaming him for the indignity. He didn't react. Which irritated her even more.

Dr. Shortt glanced at Heath. "Sorry I didn't make your brother's memorial service last month. An emergency. A near drowning." Heath nodded at the explanation, and Dr. Shortt turned his attention back to Amy, his eyes softening with the concern that she'd gotten too used to seeing in the past two months. "It would have been a difficult time for you, my dear."

At least she'd graduated to *my dear.* Then she regretted her lack of grace. "It has." Unexpected tears welled up. Frustrated, she brushed the back of her hand across her face.

"Come, let me see what's happening." Dr. Shortt looked across to where Heath stood silently by the window. "We'll be downstairs soon."

"Heath can go back to work." Amy was annoyed to hear a wobble in her voice.

Her words had the unwelcome effect of focusing that black gaze upon her. "I'm staying."

"Not in here, you're not." There was no way she was tolerating his presence while the doctor examined her.

After a moment's hesitation Heath moved to the door. "I'll wait outside."

Amy fell back against the pillows when the door closed behind him and let out a sigh of relief.

Dr. Shortt peered at her from under those bushy brows, his eyes bright and observant. "So tell me how you've been."

"Tearful." Amy gave the doctor a tremulous smile as she stated the obvious. "But that's to be expected with Roland's death, isn't it? Everyone tells me that I coped so well after it happened, and the reality is kicking in now."

The doctor humphed and produced a tympanic thermometer. "Are you sleeping?"

Sitting up and tilting her head sideways, she brushed her hair away from her ear so he could take her temperature. "I didn't the first week after Roland died. But for the last month I seem to be tired all the time." That had surprised Amy because she'd always had a lot of energy.

Another humph. He glanced at the thermometer, scrawled something on his notepad and put it away. "Young Saxon tells me that you fainted?"

Young Saxon. Heath would love that…not. But the appellation made Amy smile. "I stood up too quickly. The blood rushed to my head."

This time there was no humph as he took a cuff from his bag and soon the room was filled with the sound of pumping, until he paused to read her blood pressure. "Hmm. A little on the low side."

The first wave of fear swept her. "Is there something wrong with me?" She'd paid very little attention to herself for the last two months. Her whole life had taken on a roller-coaster quality. She no longer knew where she was going, what would happen the next day. And for a while she'd hardly cared.

"Let me examine you."

The next fifteen minutes seemed to take forever. Dr. Shortt even made her go to the adjoining bathroom and produce a specimen. A few minutes later he examined an indicator stick, looked up at her, and announced, "You're pregnant, Amy."

Horror surged through her. "I can't—" She swallowed. It *was* possible. "Are you certain?"

He didn't take umbrage at her doubt. Instead, he smiled and said, "The tearfulness, tiredness, feeling faint…they're all symptoms. Even the slightly lowered blood pressure."

"Oh, dear God." Amy covered her face. "What am I going to do?"

He asked when she'd started her last period. Amy stared at him blankly. "I had a light one and missed the next. Because of stress, I thought."

He nodded. "You need to make an appointment to have an ultrasound scan. That will give us a better idea how far along you are."

Amy dropped her hands from her face and began to chew her lip. Then she said, "I know exactly how far along I am."

The doctor nodded. "That's good. But we can confirm your suspicions. Of course, you'll also need to tell the fath—" Dr. Shortt's voice broke off and Amy knew the full enormity of the situation had finally struck him. "I'm so sorry, my dear. Did you and Roland plan to have children?"

"One day. After we were married." Not now. She'd never envisioned being a single mother. It wasn't the way Amy Wright did things. Babies were meant to come into married unions. *Ms. Wright.* How wrong was that? She wanted to weep all over again. How had she managed to screw up her life this badly?

And what was she doing using vulgar terms like *screw up?* Amy's lip started to feel tender where she'd gnawed on it.

"Your father might be able to help."

Aghast, she stared at Dr. Shortt. "My father? He's barely got enough to subsist on—there's no provision for raising a child." Despite the liquidators' gloomy forecast that her father would be broke, by some stroke of luck he'd managed to get enough out of the sale of the vineyard to buy a very modest home in nearby Hastings. "He survives day to day only by being extremely frugal."

A card was pressed into her hand. "Make an appointment to see a counsellor—it may give you some options. But, my dear, if it's any comfort to you, after so many years as a doctor I still view the conception of a baby as a miracle."

A miracle. Amy pushed the card into her pocket, her mind blank with shock. How was she going to break the news to Kay and Phillip Saxon that she, the fiancée who never took a wrong step, was about to produce their first grandchild—an illegitimate baby—outside the bonds of marriage? And even if Kay and Phillip accepted it, how could she ever forgive herself?

Heath was pacing the corridor by the time Amy and the doctor emerged from the blue guest room. He paused in midstep, his heart drumming against his ribs as he took in Amy's deathly pale face.

"What's wrong?" he asked urgently.

"I'll leave Amy to tell you." There was an incomprehen-

sible twinkle of delight in the doctor's eyes that should've reassured Heath but didn't.

One stride took him to Amy's side. "What is it?" When she
glanced away, his concern increased tenfold. "Tell me!"

"I'll see myself out, shall I?" Dr. Shortt was already halfway down the stairs before Heath belatedly remembered the
tea he'd asked his housekeeper to prepare. Too late to invite
the doctor for a cup now. "Thank you for coming, Doctor,"
he called after the departing figure.

Heath heard the front door thud close. Wrapping an arm
around Amy's stiff shoulders, he said, "Let's go down to the
living room. Josie has made a tray of tea. We'll get you a cup,
and then you can tell me what the matter is."

For a moment he thought she was going to refuse. Then she
moved, her feet dragging against the pale, thick woollen carpet.

Downstairs, once he'd settled Amy into the most comfortable armchair, Heath poured her a cup of tea and, setting it
on the small table beside her, said with an insouciance he
didn't feel, "Dr. Shortt didn't look too concerned."

"No, he considers it a miracle." Amy's tone was wooden,
her body stiffly upright in the chair.

The unfamiliar glint in her amber eyes caused his stomach
to tighten. "What miracle, Amy?" He could think of no one
who needed a miracle more.

"I'm pregnant, Heath."

For an instant a bolt of pure, blinding joy shot through
Heath. He took a stumbling, half step toward her. "Pregnant?
You're sure?"

"Yes," she snapped. "Three months' pregnant. Some
miracle. I don't want to be pregnant."

Her words sank in. *Three months' pregnant.* And then her
next statement hit him. The bottom dropped out of his
stomach…out of his world. "You mean you're going to abort
Roland's baby?"

Her eyes widened. If she'd been pale before, now she was whiter than the snow that fell on Mt. Ruapehu. "How dare you? How *dare* you believe that of me?"

Too late Heath remembered that Amy had firm, highly romantic views of family. No babies out of wedlock. White, splashy weddings with pageboys in attendance and rings on velvet cushions. Abortion wouldn't even feature. "I'm sorry," he said humbly.

She gave him a heated look. "Good."

"You're angry with me."

"Yes. No. I don't know." She bent her head and sniffed.

Oh, hell, she was about to cry again. Heath moved to kneel beside her chair.

"No," she squawked, cringing up against the padded armrest. "Stay away from me."

That annoyed Heath. Amy must know he'd never hurt her. Couldn't she understand that he only wanted to help? He rocked back on his heels to give her a little space and met her turbulent gaze squarely. "I can understand why you're angry with me."

"Can you?" She turned her head away and pursed the pink rosebud mouth that had been the subject of his most secret fantasies.

"Yes! Amy—"

"I don't want to talk about it." Folding her arms across her chest, she shrank further into herself.

Dammit, he wanted to see her eyes. He wanted to know what she was thinking. But he didn't dare touch her. Not while she was in this state. "Amy, we have to talk. We can't let this—"

"No." She was on her feet, her hands warding him off even though he hadn't moved an inch. "Take me back to work, to Saxon's Folly."

He narrowed his gaze, taking in the stiff, resentful line of her mouth, the rebellious glitter in her golden eyes. "You're not going back to work. I won't allow it."

The glitter intensified. "I am. You can't stop me."

"Of course I can," he stated through clenched teeth.

A flush of scarlet seared her cheeks. His chest contracted as her eyes grew dull and he read the despair that lay within. "You'd keep me here by force?"

The insulting implication rocked him. Heath swallowed, his mouth suddenly dry. "For God's sake, Amy, you know I'd never do that. I only meant that I wouldn't drive you back to work right now—not when you've just recovered from a faint."

Her mouth firmed. "Fine. Then I'll walk back."

"No, you won't!" Heath exploded. God, she could be irritating. Under that good-as-gold exterior lay the most stubborn little madam he'd ever met. Lowering his voice, he continued, "I don't care if it makes you angrier with me, but I'm not taking you back to work today. You fainted. You should rest. Now drink your tea while I have Josie prepare the spare room for you. You can stay the night."

The high colour leached out of her cheeks. "That is absolutely not happening!" This time Amy bolted for the front door at a run, her navy skirt tight around her legs. "I'm going back to work. I'm pregnant—not sick."

Heath caught her as she struggled with the lock on the front door and glared at her, frustration broiling inside him. Why couldn't she see that he was only trying to do what was best for her? Putting a hand out, he stopped her struggles. "So now you're an expert. What do you know about being pregnant?"

She turned her head, and he found himself gazing down into eyes as desperate as those of a trapped animal. The vulnerability he saw there shook him to the soul.

"Don't worry about me." Her shoulders sagged beneath the white shirt. "This is my problem, not yours. I'll do what Dr. Shortt said. I'll have a scan, then I'll go to an antenatal clinic… I'll find out what I need to know…I'll take vitamins. Darn it, Heath, I'm not even feeling dizzy any more."

It was true that she hadn't fainted again, and she'd promised to visit the doctor. And she was right, it wasn't his problem that she was pregnant with his brother's baby. If he told himself that often enough he might even be able to butt out.

Heath unlatched the door and stepped away, giving her the space she clearly wanted. "I'm pleased to hear you've decided to be sensible."

"And I'm pleased that you've realised I'm not staying here." Amy couldn't prevent her voice from rising as she parroted his patronizing statement back at him. *Decided to be sensible? Hah.* Her chest rose and fell as she breathed deeply and counted silently to ten. She needed to get out of here. Now. Before she fell to pieces completely. "If you won't take me back to work, then take me home."

"This was your home for many years. Why don't you pretend—"

"No." A fresh surge of panic shook her. Pretence wouldn't help…she'd tried that and it hadn't worked. It had simply gotten her deeper into the mire. And staying here would finish it off.

Amy glanced back to the sitting room, taking in the leather furniture, the bold original acrylic painting on the wall above, trying to find something final—and cutting—to say. "I don't think of this as my home any more."

If her voice hadn't wavered, it might've rung true. After all, Chosen Valley was Heath's home now, even though she'd been born and raised here. He'd taken it over, redecorated the shabby rooms. The place should have lost all familiarity. Yet it still felt warm and welcoming.

Like home…

Perhaps because the antique rocking horse she'd loved as a little girl still stood in the corner of the living room—it had been too big to take with her to the cottage she'd rented. For some reason Heath had hung on to it—probably because of its value.

For a brief instant she imagined her child riding the rocking horse. She touched her stomach and instantly the pickle of the position she found herself in came back to her. *It was not possible.* The child would not grow up at Chosen Valley.

She couldn't bear to think about any of it right now.

"Amy—"

She fixed her gaze back on Heath. "I don't want you to tell anyone that I'm pregnant."

Heath's breath caught. "Why the hell not?"

"Don't swear," she told him. "Your mother wouldn't like it." Then she realised how utterly ridiculous—how prissy— that sounded. His mother would hardly like the fact that she was pregnant, either. She shuddered with humiliation. But the only way his mother would find out was if Heath told her. Narrowing her gaze on him, she said, "I don't want you telling anyone because I'm not ready to deal with it." She couldn't bear to think of the well-meaning questions she would face, the curiosity in everyone's eyes.

"Amy—" his face softened "—whatever you believe, it's not that bad. Dr. Shortt is right: it truly *is* a miracle."

She shook her head back in rejection. "No, it's not. It's awful. It's the last thing on earth I need. Promise not to tell anyone?"

A furrow appeared between his arched brows. "You're being unreasonable. My parents will be thrilled to hear that you're pregnant with Roland's baby."

She glared at him. He couldn't possibly understand the confusion, the despair, the shame that churned inside her. No one could. "I'm *not* being unreasonable. Roland is dead. It's *my* body. My choice. *My* baby." Oh dear. She hadn't wanted to think of the life within her as belonging to her. Upset by the direction her thoughts had taken, her breathing grew ragged. "Please, Heath, just promise me."

He threw his hands into the air. "Okay, okay, if it upsets you that much I promise I won't tell."

He didn't like it; she could tell from the troubled look in his eyes. Feeling wrung out, but desperate to get out of his house, away from him, Amy said, "Please take me to my home."

Three

Abortion.

That word again. Speechless, Amy stared at the woman who'd voiced it. Carol Carter, the counsellor, was a plump middle-aged woman with dark, short hair and kind eyes that looked like they had seen too much. She'd told Carol as soon as she'd walked in that she felt confused and guilty about being pregnant out of wedlock, that it went against her core beliefs. The ease with which the counsellor suggested a solution horrified Amy.

For a moment Amy wished that she had someone beside her. Roland. Or even outspoken Megan. She needed a hand to hold, to keep her grounded.

Roland was gone. She'd never touch him again. Megan had flown out this morning to go to Australia for two days, leaving Amy five pages of notes for the summer festival.

Finally she found her voice. "I can't do that!"

"You need to consider what you're going to do." Carol's

soft voice was at odds with the harsh reality of what she was saying. "You don't have a lot of time."

"Isn't it too late for a…termination?" Amy asked. If it was too late they wouldn't need to discuss this any further.

Carol glanced down at the sheet in front of her that Amy had gotten from Dr. Shortt after her scan the previous afternoon. "There shouldn't be any risk to you if the procedure is done in the next month."

Risk to her. That made Amy feel incredibly selfish. What about the…she searched for a word, baby was too emotive…the life inside her? "No, I can't do it." She couldn't live with herself if she did that. She was healthy, physically and mentally; there was no compelling medical reason for such an extreme step.

"The fetus is nearing the end of the first trimester."

The fetus. Yes, she had to think of it as *the fetus* not *my baby.*

"Or you could consider going to term and giving the baby up for adoption." Now Carol peered over the top of her glasses, making Amy feel like a schoolkid again. "It's worth considering very seriously. You'd be giving a very special gift to a couple who want a baby."

That made her feel even worse. *She* didn't want to be pregnant. But somewhere out there another woman was desperately yearning for a baby.

The ever-lurking tears were back. *What was wrong with her?*

"Think about it," said Carol. "Given your situation and how you feel about being a single mother, it might be better for the child. Let me know what you decide."

Better for the child.

Stunned, Amy stared at the counsellor. Could she give the baby up? Even if it was in the baby's best interests? Finding out that she was pregnant had been awful. She'd resisted the idea that a baby was growing inside her, been angry, resentful. But now she was starting to accept it. She wasn't sure any longer that she could give it up for adoption. Oh, she was so confused.

When she got out of the claustrophobic white room, Heath was waiting.

Shock ripped through her. Her heart stopped for a moment at the sight of him, tall and dark, dressed all in black—the extravagant Rolex on his wrist providing the only relief—and taking up more space than he should in the reception room. "What are you doing here?"

"I saw the appointment booked into your computer. I thought you might want support." His jaw was set; he didn't look very comforting at all.

He'd stood at her desk…touched her things…checked her whereabouts on the electronic diary? Amy wrapped her arms around her stomach. "You've been spying on me."

He came closer, lifting a hand. For a moment she thought he was going to reach for her. Then his arm dropped awkwardly to his side. "Not spying—I was concerned when you didn't come to work this morning. Dad told me you'd be in late because of a doctor's appointment, but I knew you'd been to the doctor yesterday. I was worried when I heard there was another appointment."

That made her feel like a wicked, bad-tempered witch. "I'm sorry." She thought of the hand she'd craved to hold. But she didn't want Heath's hand, she wanted—

She bit her lip. "I didn't want anyone to know I was going to see a counsellor. I don't want people to think I'm losing it."

"Oh, Amy." He looked like he wanted to say more. But then he slung an arm around her shoulder and drew her close.

Instantly she grew tense.

He sighed, and his arm fell away. "Come, I'll take you back to work."

Heath was trying to take over again. "You can't give me a ride. My car is parked around the back," she objected quickly.

He nodded. "I saw it when I walked past. But you don't

look like you're in any state to drive. I'll arrange for one of the winery staff to pick it up later."

Maybe she wasn't. The compulsion to argue with him vanished. The counselling session had drained her. "You're probably right," she conceded. "I'd be better off catching a ride with you."

"Aren't I always right?" His mouth curved upward.

Amy realised that he was trying to make her laugh. But she didn't feel like she was ever going to be cheerful again. The heavy weight of the decision she had to make pressed down on her. A decision that involved not only her, but the life growing inside her as well.

But Heath didn't take her straight back to Saxon's Folly. Instead he walked her through the heart of the town to a narrow restored art deco building that housed a coffee shop, a couple of blocks from the clinic. When Amy realised his intention, her shoulders tensed and for a moment Heath thought she was going to dig her toes in and refuse to enter the crowded, popular establishment. Then she crossed the threshold and he dismissed his concern. But once seated opposite her at a table that overlooked the street, he met eyes that sparked with annoyance, and realised that Amy was even madder than he'd thought.

Belligerently, she said, "I'll have tea. Green tea. Weak."

Heath frowned. For the first time he became aware of the chattering around them and the overpowering fragrance of the specially blended coffee. "It's very crowded in here. Would you rather go somewhere else?"

"I don't want to go anywhere with you. I thought you were taking me back to Saxon's Folly."

"I want to talk to you first."

The look she gave him was intended to sting. "Did it ever cross your mind that I might not want to talk to you?"

He'd known that. But hearing her put it into words still caused an ache inside him. After the night Roland died, Amy had withdrawn. Despite all his efforts, she'd made it quite clear that she didn't want him around her.

Narrowing his eyes, he said, "That's not negotiable. We're going to talk." And he watched her bristle. Hell, it was a lot better than being treated like he didn't exist.

"About what?"

"The baby."

"Oh." She fell silent.

Heath waited, sure she would tell him it had nothing to do with him. But she remained quiet, and he took the opportunity to examine her. The pallor of yesterday was gone. She looked well, her skin glowing with a pearly sheen and her dark hair glossy. His throat closed. Amy had never looked more beautiful—or been more unattainable.

"Why are you looking me like that?"

"Like what?" he asked, buying time.

"Like I'm a bug under a microscope."

That surprised a laugh from him. "Never a bug." He hesitated, forcing himself to keep smiling at her. "I was just thinking how well you look."

She flushed.

Heath changed the subject to a safer topic. "Is the smell of the coffee in here making you feel nauseous?"

"I haven't noticed anything turning my stomach—or any cravings either." A ghost of a twinkle lit her eyes. "So you needn't feel guilty about that."

Heath gave a sigh of relief. "Thank you. At least I know that by bringing you here I haven't made you feel ill. I'm glad you're not suffering from morning sickness…or uncomfortable cravings." He smiled at her, determined that she shouldn't realise how looking at her always tugged at his heart. "Of course, that's probably partly why you never realised you were pregnant."

"I feel like such a ninny!" She yanked a toothpick out of a white porcelain holder and ripped the protective shield off. "How could I not have noticed?"

Resting his elbows on the table, Heath leaned forward. "Hardly surprising. You've had a lot on your mind."

A waitress bustled up and handed them menus and, notebook open, prepared to take their order. Heath raised an eyebrow at Amy, "Only green tea? Sure you don't want lemon cheesecake or a slice of pecan pie?"

She rolled her eyes and shook her head, so he ordered. But the waitress's arrival had broken the moment of easy cama-raderie. While they waited, Heath leaned back and watched as Amy fiddled restlessly with the wooden toothpick. She'd always been such a little thing. Finely boned. Pretty. As a child she'd attended years of ballet lessons and it showed in the way that she held herself, the graceful way she moved barely seeming to touch the ground.

Her fingers were dainty, the tips painted a soft shell-pink. Today she wore a pale pink shirt that reflected the matching hue that dusted her cheeks. An antique gold locket that always caused a little ache in his chest dangled from a gold chain just past the first button of her shirt—firmly buttoned down, of course. Her neat, bobbed hair had been pushed behind her ears and in the lobes she wore the pair of simple gold studs. From the top of her well-brushed head to her varnished toenails, Amy was a lady—the most feminine, delicate woman he'd ever met.

And if Roland hadn't died, in two weeks' time, Amy would have become Mrs. Roland Saxon.

She glanced up. Expertly, Heath wiped his face clean of all expression. He'd had a lot of practice hiding his emotions over the years.

"I forgot to tell you that your mother called yesterday morning—before I fainted," said Amy.

"Oh?" His mother had recently discovered that early in

their marriage her husband, Heath's father, had had an affair that had resulted in a child—Rafaelo, Heath's half brother. Shaken by her husband's treachery she'd left just over a week ago to stay with her brother in Australia. No one knew when she planned to returned. Heath was sorry he'd missed her. "Where was I?"

Amy shook her head. "She didn't ask for any of you. She wanted to speak to Phillip but I couldn't find him. She said she'd ring back—and asked me not to tell him."

"But you did?"

"I couldn't—I promised I wouldn't." She gave him a careful look. "I don't break promises."

And nor did he. "I won't tell Dad, either."

The waitress came back and set two steaming cups down— Amy's tea and his espresso—along with two glasses of water, and then she hurried away.

Uncertainty flashed across Amy's face. "I thought someone should know Kay had called."

"Thank you. It's been a difficult time for Mum." That was an understatement. The past couple of months had been ghastly for all of them. Roland's death in a car accident on the night of the masked ball. Rafaelo's arrival and the shocking announcement that he was Phillip's illegitimate son. He'd lost a brother...discovered a new brother. But Amy had lost the love of her life.

His eyes rested on her, and immediately she looked down at the toothpick between her fingers. "I don't know how she can bear knowing that your father betrayed her," Amy murmured.

"It's been very hard on her." Heath had seen the sadness in his mother's eyes. Rafaelo's arrival had turned her whole world upside down.

"What a terrible thing for her to discover." There was a strange note in Amy's voice; the toothpick between her fingers snapped and the splinters of wood fell from her fingers.

Heath's gaze sharpened. "Amy—" He broke off. Had Amy discovered what he'd always feared? That Roland liked to flirt—and sometimes more—with other women? Lord, he hoped not. And how could he even ask? What if he was wrong?

"Yes?" She was staring at him expectantly. There was no murky confusion in her eyes.

Amy didn't know.

He'd nearly made a terrible gaffe. Cautiously, he reached out and placed a hand over hers. "I want you to know that I don't break promises either. I told you I wouldn't tell anyone about your baby, and I won't."

Her fingers went rigid under his. "Don't call it that."

Amy's lips had barely moved. Surrounded by the anonymity of the chattering hordes, Heath had to crane forward to hear what she was saying. "What?"

"'Your baby.'" Her voice was unsteady. "Don't call it that."

Heath frowned, staring hard at her, trying to fathom what was going on in that beautiful head. "Why on earth not? It *is* your baby."

"But I don't want to think of it like that." Tears filled her eyes, sparkling like the early-morning dewdrops that collected on the vines. "Not yet. Not until I decide what I'm going to do. I don't want to grow attached to it. I don't want to love it."

Heath blinked. He hadn't fully contemplated what she must be going through. Amy had always been protective of younger kids, almost maternal. Having to make this sort of decision about her baby would be a calamity for her. He groped for something to say, but no words seemed adequately comforting…or helpful. So he tightened his fingers around hers instead.

"The counsellor suggested I consider an abortion," she said in a rush, and her throat moved visibly as she gulped.

Amy was much more upset than he'd realised. Heath wished he hadn't brought her here to this very public conversation spot, but he wasn't about to suggest that they leave. He wanted to hear what she had to say, and if they left he might not get her to open up again, might never discover her thoughts, her fears.

"What did you decide?" With his hand clamped over hers, he waited tensely for her answer. She'd been angry when he'd confronted her with the same question. Was it possible she'd changed her mind? Despite his envy of her relationship with Roland, he found he couldn't bear the thought of the last link with his brother being severed.

She shook her head and her fingers contracted under his. "I told her the same as I told you. I can't do it."

Deep inside Heath something gave, a tightness he hadn't even been aware existed. His hand gripped hers; he never wanted to let go.

Amy drew a deep breath, her fingers curling into his. "Because of my situation, she suggested I consider giving it—" Heath blinked at the emotionless pronoun but she ploughed on "—up for adoption."

He lowered his voice. "Are you considering that?"

"I don't know. I'm confused."

Her velvety eyes were naked, so vulnerable that a queer pain lodged under his breastbone. Heath wished he could absorb her agony, give her the answers she needed.

He slid his free hand under their joined fingers, cradling her hand between both of his. "You don't need to do that if you don't want to. There will be lots of people to love the baby, Amy, lots of people to help you. You won't be alone." It was a vow. He would do everything he could to make her life easier, to help her raise his brother's child.

She moved convulsively, pulling her hands free of his and spread her fingers helplessly. "What am I going to do, Heath? Under normal circumstances I'd never consider giving up my baby. But I'm not married."

"That doesn't matter—"

"It does to me," she said with a quiet dignity that made him fall silent. "And I keep remembering that Roland was adopted. Look how much joy he brought your parents. Imagine if they'd had no other children, Roland would have been their only chance. This—" her hands dropped to pat her stomach "—might do the same for another couple."

An overwhelming sense of loss shook Heath. If things had been different…if he'd been luckier…Amy's baby might have been his. Heath knew that his mother would be delighted to have a tiny piece of Roland. But he wasn't prepared to use that to blackmail Amy. She had to be content with what she decided—regardless of what everyone in his family would want. And he would support her in her decision. For him, Amy would always come first.

"Whatever you do, Amy, it must be what's right for you."

"Right for me? I've already messed that up but good. I never intended to bring a child into the world without a husband…without a father. That's my moral code. I don't know that I can bear the sideways looks, the gossip." She covered her face with cupped hands. "I suppose that makes me sound so shallow, so goody-two-shoes."

"No, it doesn't." Everyone who knew Amy knew she'd spent her life trying to do the right thing. Social conventions and good manners were important to her. She was the five-year-old who took flowers to her teacher on the first day of spring, the eight-year-old who'd never missed a day of Sunday school. At twelve she'd organized a car wash so that a classmate could dance at a competition abroad. At sixteen she'd been managing her father's house. And even now she still found time to volunteer for a string of charitable trusts.

Amy wasn't like Heath. He didn't give a rat's ass what people thought of him, but that mattered to Amy. Being bedded, unwedded and pregnant would not have been part of her life plan.

"You have to do what makes you happy. You're the one who will have to live with the decision you make now for the rest of your life."

Doubt flashed in her eyes. "That confuses me even more."

"Come." Heath pushed his chair back, the social vibe of the coffee shop suddenly unbearably oppressive. "Let's walk."

Much to his relief she didn't argue, didn't demand to be taken back to Saxon's Folly. Heath tossed a bill on the table to cover the untouched beverages.

Outside the sunlight zinged off the white art deco building on the opposite side of the road. Blinking against the bright light, Heath reached in his chest pocket for his Wayfarers.

They walked in silence. Crossing Marine Parade with a group of tourists, Heath was aware of Amy's hand swinging beside his and resisted the temptation to catch it and enfold it in his. He knew what would happen if he did—she'd withdraw back into her shell and he'd have a devil of a time getting her to talk to him again. Instead, he headed for a deserted spot where a patch of parklike green grass over-looked the black-pebbled beach and, once they were alone, he swung around to face Amy.

"Just don't do anything in a hurry, or for the wrong reasons. If you decide to give the baby up for adoption, don't do it just because Roland was adopted." The words hurt his tight throat. "You can't necessarily assume he'd want the same for his child."

Amy walked past him to the edge of the rolling grass, and stared out at the blue ocean. She looked desperately alone.

After a moment she turned back to him with a sigh that seemed wrenched from her. "I keep trying to convince myself that if I can bring myself to go through with adoption it will fulfill some other woman's dreams."

She wanted to keep the baby. Weak with relief, Heath shoved his hands in his pockets to stop himself from placing his hands on her shoulders and drawing her into the shelter of his arms. He told himself that this was Amy's decision to make, not his. But, Lord, how he wanted her to keep her baby. "You need to decide what you want—not what you think might be right for some other woman out there, but what will be right for you." Then, even though he'd told himself he wouldn't pressure her, he blurted out, "If I were the baby's father I'd selfishly hope my woman would bring the child up, share it with my family after my death, let it bring happiness back to the family."

Her brows drew together. "I'm not married, Heath. I don't have a whole lot to offer a child."

"You have us, you have Saxon's Folly." His voice dropped. "You have me."

"You?" She laughed. "You wouldn't want a child."

"I'd be there for the baby—boy or girl. If it's a boy I'll take it to cricket, to soccer." Heath found himself getting fired up. He could visualise a little boy with Amy's amber eyes and dark hair. "If it's a girl I'll screen all her boyfriends—I know precisely how the wild boys think." He grinned at her, suddenly feeling elated.

She gave him a stunned look. But he got the feeling he was getting somewhere. About time.

"I thought if I helped some couple out, if the baby was adopted out, I'd never have to tell anyone." She threw him a sideways look just as the wind ruffled her hair, giving her the look of a sea sprite. "Except for you."

She'd ask him to keep such a secret for all his life, from his family? Hadn't she learnt anything from what had happened with Roland—how much Roland's sister Alyssa had been hurt by being kept from her birth brother? But there was no point in reproaching Amy now. He had to use reason rather than emotion.

"If you decide to adopt the baby out, you'll go to term and everyone will know you're pregnant. It will be hard to miss."

She tucked her wind-fingered hair behind her ears. "They won't see. I'll tell everyone I want to go and work in Auckland, or study or something. I can't stay here whatever I decide to do about the baby. Even if I keep it, it will be better for me to start over in Auckland."

"Start over in Auckland?" Her announcement came like a fist in the groin. This was a complication he hadn't foreseen. All these years he'd at least been able to see her, even if she had been pledged to his brother. "You'd run away?"

"It won't be running away. I just can't stay here."

"Why not? Lots of women get pregnant, have babies out of wedlock. No one bats an eyelash any more."

"Not me."

Steel underpinned those quiet words. With a growing sense of panic, Heath knew that on this he wouldn't be able to sway her. Whatever she decided, Amy was going to leave.

And he would lose her. Forever.

Four

"There's another solution."

Heath stood with his back to the sun, his arms folded across his chest, eyes hidden by the dark shades, his face impossible for Amy to read.

"There is?" Amy gave him an uncertain smile, relief unfurling within her. She was all out of ideas about how to get out of this horrible totally un-Amy-like mess that she'd managed to land herself in.

"You could marry me."

That knocked the breath out of her. The smile withered and she simply stared at him. Then she whispered, "Marry you?"

His mouth slanted. "Is it such a terrible proposition? Please tell me you're not about to faint again."

"No, I'm not going to faint." But his suggestion made her head spin. She stumbled away from him to where the grass met pebble and gazed out again at the Pacific. The water was incredibly blue and the moist breeze smelled of salt and sun.

An idyllic scene. Yet eighty years ago the ocean in front of her had been violently shaken by an earthquake. Right now Amy felt as though her whole familiar world had tumbled upside down. *Heath offering to marry her?*

It was insane.

"Why?" she whispered, then realised he wouldn't hear her. She turned, to find him standing right behind her. He had taken the sunglasses off, and his eyes narrowed as they met hers. Gooseflesh broke over her upper arms, and she rubbed her hands up and down them, suddenly cold despite the summer sunshine.

"Because you don't want to have a baby without being married."

"But that's my problem, not yours," Amy objected, squinting against the bright light of the Hawkes Bay and noticing for the first time that despite the upward slant of his mouth, his eyes were intense. Watchful. She glanced away from the piercing look and took in the tightly coiled stance that belied the lulling, reasonable tone of his voice.

"Roland was my brother," he said softly. "This will be his only child."

"He wouldn't expect you to sacrifice yourself for his baby." Amy had a sneaky feeling that Roland would never have done that for Heath if their positions had been reversed. She hurriedly banished the traitorous thought.

"It wouldn't be a sacrifice." There was a peculiar note in his voice.

"Of course it would! You've always said that you'll never marry—you even said it to me just a few days ago."

He nodded. "True. But circumstances have changed since then."

"What's changed?" she challenged.

"You need a husband—"

"I don't *need* a husband!" That made her sound so weak. Like some simpering female living in Victorian times.

"I mean—" Heath was scowling "—you need a father for your child. You're never going to be happy being a single mother."

Amy thought about that and nodded slowly. "Correct. I believe that in a perfect world babies belong in families." But her world was no longer perfect. It had been disrupted, turned on its head by a series of events totally out of her control.

"So marry me. We'll be a family."

He didn't move, yet Amy had the feeling he was willing her to say Yes. The strength of his power was overwhelming. "Why do you want this so badly?"

His scowl grew blacker. "I don't 'want this so badly.'"

The sudden distance between them hurt Amy in places that she hadn't thought were susceptible to hurt any more. She chewed her lip and stayed silent.

With a sigh Heath rubbed his hand over the back of his neck and said, "It seems like a way of solving all our problems."

"My problems maybe." Amy tilted her head and assessed him. Although hot-tempered, Heath had always sauntered through life with a don't-care swagger. Little seemed to matter to him. Sure, he worked hard, and the aura of success he wore with casual disregard didn't hurt. Nor did his effortless natural charm. He had lots of friends and few people cared to be his enemy—mostly due to the big-fighter, hell-raiser reputation of his youth. "*You* don't have any problems." At least none that she knew about.

"You think not?" There was that edge that made her so uneasy.

"You're successful…"

His mouth twisted. "So being rich and hardworking means I don't have problems?"

That made her sound superficial, as though she was incapable of seeing under life's surface. "You don't work *that* hard," she defended her opinion.

"Ah, so I'm just rich and lucky…maybe even a little lazy?"

"I never said you're lazy." But she'd thought it. Just as she'd thought he was incredibly fortunate. Everything he wanted always seemed to just fall into Heath's lap with little effort. Success, great harvests…fine-boned, beautiful women. Could she have been wrong about him? Amy shifted uncomfortably. "Can we change the subject please?"

She moved away, to a bench positioned to take advantage of the expansive sea view, and sank down.

Heath followed, dropping down beside her. He turned his body to face her, placing his arm negligently along the back of the wooden bench. "No, this is getting interesting. So what else do you think of me?"

"You're charming. People like you." She looked at him— really looked at him for the first time in her life. From this close up, his body was solid and compact with muscle under the black jeans and black button-down shirt. The undone top button revealed a wedge of tanned skin. Above that his jaw was granite-hard, his cheekbones high and slanted, and his eyes glittered. No wonder women always stopped to stare at him. "You're good-looking."

The last came in a rush, and to her mortification Amy felt herself flush.

"Charming. Popular. Good-looking." The dark eyes flattened with displeasure. "Hardly sterling character traits."

With a start, Amy realised he was angry. "I didn't mean to offend you."

"No matter." His lips barely moved. "You're always so polite. It's interesting to learn what you really think of me under the exquisite manners."

"You're taking this all wrong—"

"I worked damn hard to pull the vineyard out of the mess your father left it in, Amy. I planted thousands of new vines— many with my own hands. It was a day-and-night job for weeks…months." He paused. "If you didn't see me for months, that's what I was doing." His mouth twisted. "Not partying nonstop."

Was he simply underscoring how wrong her perception of him as a hell-raiser had been? Or was that a dig at the frenetic over-the-top way Roland had romanced her?

She examined him but couldn't find anything to support the suspicion. Her hand crept to the gold locket around her neck. "You know my father never allowed me to be involved with the business." He'd expected her to fill her life with ladylike pursuits. Reading. Shopping. Volunteer duties. "But the estate couldn't have been in such bad shape. Dad always—"

"It was bankrupt."

He didn't say more, but the hard line of his mouth told her that he spoke the truth. Amy glanced away. In front of her the ocean moved lazily—calm today—and to one side a territorial seagull shrieked, chasing another along the stony beach. But all she could see was the expression of dismay on the face of the bank manager when she'd gone to see him with a financial plan to run a bed-and-breakfast to help ease her father's financial burden. He'd turned her down flat. Told her that she'd need someone to stand as guarantor before the bank would even consider throwing good money after bad.

Then Heath had come in with an offer to buy Chosen Valley Winery lock, stock and barrel. She'd resented the ease with which he'd had those same bankers fawning over him. And, irrationally, she'd resented the fact that she'd never had the opportunity to save her father—and herself.

"I knew it wasn't good, but I didn't know it was that bad," she said at last, steeling herself to meet his gaze.

"You thought I'd scored a bargain?" His eyebrows shot up. "I paid more than I should've for what I got." He shut his mouth, clearly annoyed with himself for saying that much.

"If it had happened now I might have been able to help Dad save it. I've learned so much about the industry since working for Saxon's Folly." And she owed him for that job. She softened her tone, "Thanks, Heath."

"I don't want your gratitude." His hands balled into fists at his sides, his eyes seething with suppressed frustration.

"I'm sorry," she said in a small voice.

"Oh, Amy." He closed his eyes. When he opened them the heat was gone. "It's not you I'm angry with, it's myself."

"Why?"

"For the chaos I've caused."

"Your life isn't chaotic—you've got everything anyone would want."

"I caused no end of trouble as a youngster. I barely have a relationship with my father, and I know that upsets my mother."

"But they love you."

He shrugged. "Perhaps. I nearly alienated Rafaelo—I thought he was a fake. I didn't recognise my own half brother—"

"He could've been a con man."

"Thank you." He gave her the first trace of his killer smile. "And I was always far too critical of Roland when he was alive."

At this last addition to the catalogue of his sins, Amy stared blindly at the Pacific. She considered not answering, but honesty propelled her to whisper, "Maybe he deserved it."

Heath let out an audible breath. "That's why you need to marry me. When I left Saxon's Folly and first bought Chosen Valley, Dad was furious. He said a lot of things in anger—and one was that he'd never forgive me for going into competition with him, that I should never hope to come back to Saxon's Folly."

"But you are back."

"Not because my father asked. Because Caitlyn begged me, and because Joshua convinced Dad it was the sensible thing to do in the short term."

That brought her eyes back to his face. "The short term?"

"I'm on trial, Amy. And I need to get on with Dad to stay."

"Do you want to stay?"

Heath hesitated. "Yes. With all that's happened in the last two months I know now that there are no guarantees in life." Amy knew he was talking about Roland's tragic death. And perhaps even about the chasm that had opened between his mother and father with Rafaelo's arrival. "I want to heal the breach with my father."

"I can understand that." Another thought struck her. "Does that mean you'll be selling Chosen Valley?"

He shook his head. "Chosen Valley is my home now. I can be winemaker for both estates."

"Won't there be a conflict of interest?"

"No, the focus of the estates is different. I'm concentrating more on growing reds. But I need you to help me convince my father that I'm back for good, that I won't walk out again. My parents adore you—you're their favourite godchild, and they have several."

She threw him a smile, her normal cheerfulness starting to return. "It's only because my mum and Kay were best friends— and because I lived close by when I was growing up. They saw more of me than their other godchildren."

"It's not only that—you're part of the family."

Her heart warmed and her smile widened. "That's a lovely thing to say, Heath. But I'm worried they'll think less of me if they find out I…"

"Slept with Roland before the wedding?"

She gave a jerky nod, her smile fading.

Heath waved a hand dismissively. "With all the skeletons that have fallen out of their closets recently, they're hardly in the position to throw stones. And if it matters to anyone, then they're not true friends. My parents do love you."

Maybe Heath was right. Who would care? She was allowing her own scruples to overwhelm her.

He was staring at her intently, his mouth curving into a

genuine smile that made her feel like the most appreciated woman on the planet.

Amy shifted on the hard wooden bench again. Uncomfortable, but in a different way. Why had she never noticed until today how devastatingly good-looking Heath was?

Because she'd been engaged to Roland. Because she'd written Heath off as a bad boy—not her type. Because she'd been blind.

The warmth that his gaze had ignited rushed through her, coursing along her veins, pooling deep in her belly. *Stop this!* She told herself. *It's silly.*

"I'm very fond of your parents, too. It would be sad if they decided to separate."

Heath gave her a narrowed look. "If you marry me perhaps the news of the baby will help heal the wounds."

Her breath snagged in her throat. "They'd wonder why you were marrying me. Wouldn't they ask if it was your baby?" The air seemed to dry up, and distress caused her breath to escape in shallow gasps. "I couldn't bear that. I'd be so humiliated."

There was a hostile gleam in Heath's black gaze. "Don't worry. I'd make sure they never doubted that you're carrying Roland's baby, not mine."

Amy's heart started to pound. "You'd do that?"

After a pulsing moment he nodded.

"I'd hate them—or anyone—to think I betrayed Roland." She couldn't meet his bitter gaze. She stared determinedly at her fingernails. The polish on her right index finger had chipped. She needed to redo the varnish tonight.

"No one would think it, Amy. You've always done the right thing. No one would ever suspect you of sleeping with your fiancé's brother."

The savage note in his voice brought her eyes to his face. A muscle was leaping in his cheek.

A desperate need to escape closed in on her. She jumped

to her feet. "I just want to do the right thing for my baby," she said faintly.

My baby.

She closed her eyes. Oh, no. She hadn't wanted to bond with the life inside her, hadn't wanted to grow to love it—not if she was going to lose it, or give it away.

But now she had a chance to consider keeping it.

Though it would mean marrying Heath.

Did she dare?

She put her hand over her belly. The slight swelling was barely noticeable to her touch. Nothing obvious enough yet to reveal that she was pregnant. She certainly didn't feel like she was carrying a baby. It all seemed so unreal. Everything was happening too quickly.

"Marrying me will be the right thing to do, Amy." Heath had risen and stood beside her. She was so aware of his every move and the even sound of his breathing overpowered the suck of sea on the pebbles. "You'll see. Everyone will be delighted about your pregnancy."

With a gesture of bravado she lifted her chin and met those ebony eyes. "Can I think about it?"

"Take all the time you want. But remember, this baby is a Saxon and Roland was proud to be a Saxon. This is what he'd want for the baby."

Heath wanted marriage so that he could get a second chance with his family. So that his parents would forget their differences and, comforted by their first grandchild, be able to recover from the grief of losing their son.

As for her, she'd get to keep the baby…and she hadn't dared let herself think of that possibility before now.

Her baby.

A little being that was all hers that she could love with all her heart. A baby that would grow up at Chosen Valley, her childhood home. It all made perfect sense. Except…

Except there would be no love between her and Heath.

* * *

Marry Heath or move to Auckland.

It was an impossible choice. Amy glanced up and down the dining table in the Saxon's long formal dining room and the indecision that had been twisting her stomach into knots for the past two days intensified. At the head of the table sat Heath's father, Phillip, with Amy and Joshua's fiancée, Alyssa, on either side of him. Joshua sat on Amy's left with Heath opposite him.

Heath had picked her up early this evening. With Megan away for the past two days, the Saxons' usual Thursday evening gathering had been moved to Friday.

Since he'd collected her, Heath hadn't mentioned his proposal and Amy had been exceedingly grateful. *What was she going to decide?* Cutting into the chicken Maryland on her plate, Amy studiously avoided meeting Heath's gaze and pretended to listen with fascination to the three-way conversation between Joshua, Phillip and Alyssa about a Saxon Folly wine that was garnering rave reviews, while she was acutely aware of Heath sitting so silently on the other side of the table.

"Heath, I've been meaning to tell you, I had a call from the police today," said Joshua.

The police? Amy started to pay attention.

Heath set down his fork. "About the young thugs that caused Alyssa's fall? Or the fire in the stables?"

Alyssa's hand had been hurt in a fall from a horse. Joshua had blamed himself. Then only last month the stables had been set ablaze. Caitlyn had risked her life to rescue the horses. The police had suspected arson.

"Both. They've made an arrest," Joshua continued, "It would appear that the cases are linked."

"Who would do such a terrible thing?" The malice of it all stunned Amy.

"The police arrested someone called Carson Smith—turns out he's the younger brother of Tommy Smith."

"Tommy Smith?" Amy knew she should recognise the name. But she couldn't place it.

"He used to work at Saxon's Folly—Joshua fired him. And rightly so." Heath's voice was hard, his mouth tight at the memory.

Of course! Amy wanted to bang her palm against her forehead. A distressed Kay had once told her in deepest confidence that Tommy had assaulted Caitlyn…that if Joshua hadn't arrived and stepped in, who knew how far the attack might have gone.

Phillip was nodding as Joshua explained. "Young Carson blamed the Saxons for sending Tommy to jail. Now he will be facing charges for arson and assault—he admitted to knocking the guard out that night, too. He knew that Caitlyn lived in the loft above the stables, so there may well be an attempted murder charge, too."

Amy drew a deep breath. "Does Caitlyn know yet?"

"I've already called Rafaelo to update him," said Joshua. "He was ready to come back and sort the guy out himself." Joshua's mouth slanted in a wry grin. "I told him he was better off spending the time introducing Caitlyn to Spain."

That lightened the mood and the talk moved on to Spanish wines and sherries.

Amy took a mouthful of food and let the conversation wash over her. Megan hadn't yet arrived and Amy was also conscious of the empty spaces further down the long, refectory-style table. The chair that Roland always used had been pushed back against the wall, and a pang of sorrow pierced her at the sight. And there were other spaces too: Rafaelo and Caitlyn were in Spain, of course, while Alyssa occupied Kay's place now that Kay was in Australia.

If she didn't accept Heath's proposal, then soon she would

be gone, too. Amy knew she couldn't afford to wait too long to make her decision. This morning she'd noticed that the cups of her bra were tight and her breasts had developed a painful sensitivity. It wouldn't be long before the telltale signs started to show.

But it would be hard settling in a big city like Auckland after living in the Hawkes Bay all her life. She was a country girl at heart. She'd have to tender her resignation, tell the Saxons…her father…of her decision to leave. And then cut all ties for the next six to eight months.

Running away, Heath had called it. She didn't dare look at him, even though she was aware of every movement he made, the strength in his tanned hand as he buttered a roll, the grace of his movements as he lifted his glass to his lips.

What was she to do?

Amy stabbed her fork at a piece of chicken. Heath had said that her baby was a Saxon, that it belonged here. Deep down Amy knew the baby deserved to know its grandparents, to play in the Victorian homestead and roam the vineyards and hear the tales about the infamous Joseph Saxon, the first owner of Saxon's Folly.

Yet how could she marry a man she didn't love? A man with no hint of softness, a man she'd never understand?

It was a relief when Megan rushed in, cell phone in hand, her eyes bright and cheeks flushed.

"Sorry I'm late. I lost track of time. I'm still on Australian time." Megan plunked herself down beside Heath. "Joshua, can I have a glass of that, please?"

Joshua rose to his feet, uncorking the bottle, and the gurgle of the liquid filling Megan's glass was loud in the sudden silence. He moved to fill Amy's glass.

"No, thanks." She whipped the glass out of his reach.

"You have to try it," Joshua said. "It's a Riesling, sharp and drier than usual. It's superb."

"I'm not drinking wine at the moment." Dr. Shortt had been firm about that.

"You're not trying to lose weight?" Joshua said in a tone of brotherly scolding.

"Joshua!" Alyssa gave her fiancé a look that boded ill. "Leave Amy alone."

"Josh is right." Megan added her voice to the debate. "You need to add a couple of pounds—not lose more."

The weight had dropped off her slight frame in the weeks after Roland's death. But the mother-hen note in Megan's voice and all the gentle chiding made Amy want to scream. "I'm not trying to lose more weight," she said tersely.

"I mean, it's not as if you're pregnant or anything," Megan said airily.

Amy felt herself reddening.

It was Megan who tactlessly made the connection first, her gaze homing in on Amy. "Or are you?"

There was an appalled silence. Then Heath thundered, "Megan, that's enough!"

"Oh, my God." Megan's hand covered her mouth and her eyes bugged out at Amy over the top.

In utter devastation, Amy shut her eyes. She couldn't bear to look at anyone. She knew guilt must be written all over her in neon-bright colour.

Megan's timid "I'm so sorry, Amy," broke her stasis.

With a shudder she opened her eyes and faced the family she'd known all her life. "I suppose you had to find out sometime." But it didn't help the sick churning in her stomach.

"Congratulations." Alyssa was grinning at her, and Joshua stretched an arm around the back of her chair and enveloped her in a great bear hold.

Over Joshua's forearm Amy could see Phillip Saxon beaming with a joy she hadn't seen for months.

"That's wonderful news, Amy. A baby." He paused, his

eyes blurring. "Roland's baby. Kay is going to be just as thrilled as I am."

Amy gulped, her throat burning with the effort to hold back the tears of humiliation and emotion that threatened to overwhelm her. She wasn't going to cry. She'd shed enough tears in the past two months to last a lifetime. She wriggled free of Joshua's hold and gave Heath a desperate, pleading look across the table. *Help me,* she wanted to yell at him. But after one flash of unreadable emotion his features froze.

There was no hint of *I told you* so in his face. But he had— he'd told her how important this baby would be to his family. She'd simply been too dim, too shattered, to fathom why.

A miracle.

Her baby was a way to get a part of Roland back into their blighted lives.

Five

Heath floored the accelerator and the Lamborghini roared down the long lane, away from Saxon's Folly. The silence that lay between him and Amy cut into the night.

Amy had turned her head away and was staring out into the darkness, making no effort to share her thoughts about what had happened back at Saxon's Folly, but he knew her well enough to know that she would've been mortified.

Yet he had absolutely no idea how she was going to react.

And that scared him.

His mouth pursed into a tight, contained line, Heath stared into the darkness beyond the headlights. He knew there was a strong possibility that his sister's tactless blunder might jolt Amy into turning his proposal down and fleeing to Auckland.

Only minutes later, Heath rolled down the narrow lane that passed through the small seaside village of Hedeby. Aside from the huddle of cottages, there was only a general dealer cum post office and a fish-and-chips takeout store. The shops were in darkness and only a few lights still glimmered through wind-thinned hedges.

The throaty roar of the powerful sports car cut out beside the white timber cottage that was now Amy's home. Already she was reaching for the door handle.

"Not so fast."

Her shoulders hunched for a second. Then she turned to face him, her face a pale blur in the night. "Yes?"

"What have you decided?"

"You want an answer now?"

Heath knew it was a mistake to push her. But dammit he didn't want to go through any more of the endless waiting that had been driving him crazy.

"I think you need to make a decision as soon as possible now that the news is out."

"The news that I'm pregnant with your brother's baby?" She made a raw sound. "It's worse than I'd imagined. I've never been so…"

"I know. You're humiliated. I could wring my sister's neck."

"It's not Megan's fault," she said with commendable loyalty.

Heath snorted. "Of course it is. She's always had a serious case of foot-in-mouth disease."

But Amy didn't laugh. "Soon everyone will know."

"Who cares?" he asked.

"I do." Amy drew a shuddering breath. "That's the difference. I'm not you, Heath. Things like this matter to me."

He sighed. It had been a long time since people's opinions mattered to him—bar a few. But Amy was wrong. There *were* things that mattered to him. The important stuff. Like Amy and her baby. "It will be a nine-day wonder, and then something new will come along for everyone to gossip about."

"Yes, but for nine days the main topic will be me." She sounded resentful. "I want my ordered life back."

"A baby's going to ruin that anyway." She'd be alone, coping by herself. It wouldn't be easy.

"It's not the baby that would ruin it." Amy put her fingers to her temples. "I always wanted a baby."

Heath had a vision of Amy holding her baby, smiling down at the shape swaddled in her arms. But the taller figure he envisioned in the background wasn't Roland...

She was speaking again. He jerked his attention back to what she was saying.

"But the babies were supposed to come after the marriage. Not like this." Amy gripped her purse and closed her eyes.

He was furious at his irresponsible brother...at Amy for not seeing Roland for what he was...and at himself for being an unwilling participant in the whole mess that had been made of Amy's life.

"So marry me." He hadn't meant to ask again but the words burst from him. "I'll take care of you—and the baby. We can go away for a nine-day honeymoon. By the time we get back all the stir will be over." He had a vision of every person Amy knew lining up to greet them on their return, eyes agog with avid speculation, and he started to laugh.

"It's not funny, Heath."

"It's not as bad as you think, either. Relax. Say Yes. I promise you, no one will dare say a word with me around. I won't let them."

"You're right. No one will dare."

He didn't want her to marry him because of his formidable reputation as a fighter, but he'd take every advantage he could. "Is that a yes?"

The faint light in the car glinted in her eyes. Heath tensed as she made a little fluttering movement with her hands.

Then she sighed. "What choice do I have? Okay, I'll marry you, Heath."

* * *

After accepting Heath's proposal, Amy found events moving at the speed of light. She'd hardly drawn a breath, and Heath was studying the calendar on his BlackBerry for a suitable wedding date and talking about arranging caterers.

Before she could beg him to slow down, give her breathing space and a chance to get used to the idea, Kay Saxon came home.

The first indication that Amy had of Heath's mother's return was the click of heels across the stone floor of the winery.

"Amy, darling." Kay burst into the space behind the counter and engulfed Amy in a lavender-scented hug. "Heath called to say that you're expecting Roland's baby…and that you two are getting married. How can I ever tell you how much this means to me?" Kay set her away, her eyes brimming with tears. "You should have told me sooner about the baby."

"I didn't know myself." A sense of being trapped closed around Amy. Leaning across her desk, she tore a tissue from the box and handed it to Kay.

"I don't know why I'm crying. I never cry." Kay wiped her eyes and stared down at the streaks of moisture on her fingertips. Then she gave Amy a brilliant smile. "They must be tears of happiness."

If Amy hadn't already agreed to marry Heath she knew that Kay's tears—and that ecstatic smile—would have sealed her fate. *She had no choice.* "You don't mind?" she asked in a small voice.

"Mind?" Kay gave her a questioning look. "Why should I mind?"

"You don't think this looks…well…bad?" Amy coloured, uncomfortable at the awkwardness of what she had to say. "That people will say that I was supposed to marry Roland and now I'm marrying Heath?"

Kay waved a hand. "Who cares what people think? It's the

baby that matters. I'm proud of Heath for doing what had to be done, and of you for recognising that it was the sensible thing. You're both behaving with great responsibility."

Sensible? How could anything about this farce be remotely described as sensible? As for responsible…if Kay only knew. The sick churning in her stomach grew worse.

"You do realise what this means?" Kay was asking.

Amy shook her head.

"It means that any thought I had of divorcing Phillip and staying in Australia is out of the question." Kay smoothed a hand over her immaculate hair. "I need to be here near you— and Roland's baby."

For a wild moment Amy thought she was going to faint again. She drew a long, steadying breath. "You can't go to Australia, Kay. You love it here."

"I could hardly stay once I'd divorced Phillip."

Did that mean Kay was no longer considering a divorce? Amy didn't dare ask. Instead she said breathlessly, "I'd love to have your help with the baby."

"I wonder if the baby will have bright red hair like Roland—or dark auburn hair like his sister?" Kay mused.

Red hair? Her heart slammed against her ribs. Oh, good gracious. She hadn't thought about what her baby would look like. "It might have my dark hair."

Footsteps scraped on the floor on the other side of the counter. Measured, male footsteps. *Oh, no! Not now.* Amy raised her head with a sense of inevitability.

Heath stood there looking oddly formal in a dark suit, watching them both, his face inscrutable. Amy couldn't help the once-over she gave him. He wore no tie, the top button of his white shirt was undone. In that brief second she took in everything about him, before giving him an awkward smile. "Heath, your mother's back—and all because of the baby."

"And the news of your engagement," said Kay happily.

As Heath came forward, the whole mood in the winery changed. There was a sudden burst of energy, of expectant excitement. Amy had never noticed how tall he was, how commanding. How could she have missed it?

"Welcome home, Mum."

Going around the counter, Kay flung her arms around his neck. "I missed you—all of you. I'm so pleased to be home. Isn't Amy's news fabulous? Your father is so pleased, too."

Over his mother's head he met Amy's gaze. He might as well have said, "See? My family *needs* this baby."

The sense of suffocation increased. Amy knew that all he cared about was the baby in her womb—and what it could do to heal the hurts in his family.

Once again, the awareness of his ruthlessness shook her. Oddly nervous, she stroked the filmy fabric of the pink dress she wore down over her hips, her hands suddenly clammy. Would she be able to retain her sense of self in their marriage? Or would she become no more than a vessel that carried a Saxon baby?

"Oh, what a good idea." Kay was clapping her hands together.

Confused, Amy stared at Heath. "Sorry? I missed that."

"Heath's going to take you out for lunch. To celebrate." For a moment Kay's eyes clouded. Amy could read her thoughts as clear as day.

Roland should be here to do that.

Guilt twisted inside her. She shoved it aside. No time for that now. "I've got work to do. I'm not sure—"

"It will be good for you to get out." Heath's tone was even.

"I'll call Voyagers, see if dear Gus can spare you a table, that's the very place where I told Phillip I was pregnant with Joshua." Kay's eyes were alight with joy. "Don't worry, Amy darling, I'll man reception while you're gone."

Amy knew when she was beaten. "That sounds lovely."
But she glared at Heath through dagger-sharp eyes.

At Voyagers the rich patina of the proprietor's Nordic
ancestry clung to the light-coloured European hardwood floor-
boards and the linen sails that covered the courtyard outside.

Once Amy and Heath had been seated inside at a table beside enormous sash windows that overlooked the busy
Marine Parade with the Pacific glistening in the sunshine
beyond, they ordered from the menu of daily specials, which
Gus guaranteed were made with the freshest ingredients he
could source.

When the food arrived, Amy's Cajun chicken salad was to
die for and Heath's steak looked equally good. They talked
about the history of the Hawkes Bay and the assortment of
cultures that had landed there—like Gus's family who had
arrived in Napier in the late 1800s. It was fascinating. And,
for once, Amy found that conversation with Heath went rela-
tively easily with no awkward silences.

But after the meal, when his coffee and her tea arrived
along with a plateful of chocolate mints, that all changed.
Heath sat back and his dark suit jacket parted to reveal the
breadth of his chest under the white cotton business shirt, a
small triangle of skin exposed by the undone top button. Amy
jerked her gaze away from that distracting bit of skin when
Heath said, "There's one thing we have to talk about, Amy."

Her heart dropped through the bottom of her stomach at
the unaccustomed gravity in his black-devil's eyes. Full of
trepidation, she asked, "What?"

"Sex."

That single, sizzling word landed in the space that separated them like a primed-to-explode hand grenade. Amy
could feel the blood draining from her face. "No, I don't want
to talk about—"

"We have to." His voice was strangely gentle. He shrugged the jacket off his shoulders onto the chair behind him, as if he too had experienced a wave of heat. "We're going to be married. You can't expect me not to want to make love to my wife."

Make love.

Her body sagged.

There wouldn't be any love involved. She liked Heath. Once upon a time they'd even been friends—but love? Never. He was her extreme opposite, bad boy to her good girl. They had nothing in common.

Especially not love.

All they had was the baby, whispered a little voice. And Chosen Valley. Wasn't that more than a lot of people started with?

And there was the little fact that she was highly aware of him. He aroused feelings in her she'd never experienced. Sex with Heath would be no hardship. Amy swallowed convulsively. Animal attraction, for sure. She dismissed the irritating voice. No way was she admitting that.

"I—" She broke off. Tried again. "I don't think…" Her voice trailed away.

"You won't have to think, Amy." Heath's dark eyes smiled at her. "Only feel."

The blush took her by surprise. Wild colour suffused her cheeks, her breasts, her whole body under the candy floss pink dress, causing her to feel hot and twitchy. "Heath!"

His wicked smile faded and his expression turned serious. "I don't want a sexless marriage, Amy. And I don't want you to fool yourself that I'd ever settle for that."

Settle for…

Oh, good grief. As far as Heath was concerned he'd be settling for enough already. His brother's woman, his brother's baby. That brought up another problem. "What if you fall in love with someone else?"

"That's not going to happen."

He sounded so very certain. Amy badly wanted to believe him. "Is that why you've never married? Because you've never been in love?"

The beautiful male mouth twisted. "Something like that."

Amy eyed him, feeling as if she was missing something. But his ironic expression warned her that she might not like the answers if she forced the issue. Yet she needed to be sure.

"If you do fall in love—if it hits you like lightning—then what?"

His lips curved into what should've been a smile, if the expression in his eyes hadn't been so flat. "It's not going to happen. I'm not the susceptible type."

Amy inspected him. His chest was broad and his biceps bulged under the sleeves of the fine cotton shirt he wore. She'd seen the stream of women through his life. Petite. Pretty. Predictably interchangeable. "But you've always had girlfriends."

"I've never fallen in love with any of them."

Maybe not, but several had fallen in love with him. Poor, stupid women. "What's to stop you from having more?" A fine strand of tension wound up inside her and she watched him carefully. She didn't think she could bear it if her husband had other women. That was one of the reasons she and Roland—

"My marriage." His answer interrupted her thoughts.

"You're telling me you'd be faithful?" Amy knew she sounded disbelieving. It was more than she deserved. But if he wanted a real marriage—with sex and all the trimmings—she'd need to be sure of his fidelity.

He nodded.

"I'd expect fidelity if we were—" The flush crept over her again.

"Having sex?"

She gulped at his frankness. Her face must be as red as a beet. "Er…yes," she stuttered.

"You've got it."

Amy stared, gobsmacked. She'd expected more of a struggle to get his agreement. And that made her feel as if the rug had been pulled out from under her. Again.

Determined to regain a little ground, Amy lifted her chin and said, "And there's something else we need to talk about."

Heath raised an eyebrow.

She hesitated. If he could say *sex*, then so could she. "Sexual health."

"You're worried about your health then?"

"Me?" Amy stared. "You think I—" Words failed her.

"You slept with my brother. If he compromised his health, you were at risk."

Amy didn't like the idea that one reckless night that she bitterly regretted might have cost her so much. She'd been incredibly stupid.

"I'll have some tests done," she said decisively.

Heath's gaze dropped to her belly. "I hope it's not too late for that. My brother was a lot less discriminating than I am."

Given her doubts, that stung.

"Why should I believe that?" Amy said heatedly. "Everyone knows you're the bad boy. Black Saxon they call you."

Only the slightest flicker showed that he'd registered her taunt. "Not in that respect—you can check with Dr. Shortt. I don't take risks."

Heath not take risks? Hard to believe. He'd always pushed every boundary he could with his wild behaviour. But his gaze was level and Amy found herself believing him. Inwardly she gave a deep sigh of relief.

"I don't need to ask Dr. Shortt," said Amy.

"You should. You're entitled to a clean bill of health from a soon-to-be lover."

Her pulse started to thud. "If you give me your word, that's enough," she said a trifle hoarsely.

All Heath's attention was fixed on her. "I give you my

word. You can trust me." There was a strange note in his voice. "I've always been careful…for myself and my partners. And I've never done one-night stands."

Now that was stretching it too far. Amy snorted. "Never? Not once?"

He looked uncomfortable. "Maybe once."

"I knew it!"

When Heath started to say something Amy interrupted him with a change of subject. "What if the baby's born…starts calling you Daddy…and then you decide you want out the marriage?"

"I won't want out."

"You might get bored."

He showed his teeth in a smile that wasn't very comforting at all. "I won't get bored."

Amy shifted, uncomfortable, a little nervous, and a whole lot unsettled. She wasn't sure she understood him any more. He was so alien, so closed off. And everything he said seemed to have an edge, making her feel as if there was something that she was missing.

She hadn't liked that feeling when she'd been fourteen and the other girls had giggled about stuff that good girls like Amy knew nothing about. Stuff about bad boys and French kissing. Well, she was grown up now and pregnant to boot and yet she still had that embarrassing sense of missing half the conversation.

So she took cover by trying to look like she didn't feel stupid. She stuck her nose in the air and said in her most snooty, disbelieving tone, "You always said you never wanted to get married—so how can you say it wouldn't bore you?"

His gaze narrowed until only a glitter of granite showed. "I told you, things change. I might not have wanted to get married before, but now I do."

The feeling something was eluding her intensified. She stared back at him, trying to read what was going on behind that hard-boned face. "Because of the baby?"

After a long moment he nodded. "Yes, because of the baby."

Amy hadn't wanted Heath to agree with her. She'd wanted him to object, to argue. She'd wanted to gain some insight into what she was starting to realise was a labyrinthine mind. Heath was a lot more complex than the bad boy she'd written him off as. But she was growing weary of being nothing more than a vessel for a Saxon baby. She wanted to talk about herself and Heath…and the future. To gauge what the chances were of this marriage between them working.

With a touch of frustration she said, "Well, if we both want what's best for the baby, then I expect everything will work out."

"It won't be that easy, Amy." That edge was still there under the slight smile. "We'll have to work at our marriage."

He'd moved closer.

She felt breathless. Her skin started to tingle, and all at once the light seemed brighter, the scent of the gardenias in the gigantic glazed pots in the courtyard grew more heady. His face took up her full vision. His eyes were dark, brooding, his cheekbones forming a hard ridge under his face. He looked downright dangerous.

Blood pounded through her head. Consciously she let out the breath she'd been holding and the pounding eased a little, but the strange flutter in her stomach didn't subside.

Excitement, she realised with a sense of shock.

Amy looked quickly away, before he could read what she was feeling.

"Amy…" Heath paused.

Tension filled the air. Against her will, her eyes slid back. A small black-velvet box lay on the white linen tablecloth next to Heath's tanned hand. Amy's mouth went dry. The moment of reckoning had arrived. She stared at the dainty box, making no move to pick it up.

"Open it," urged Heath.

Six

Amy lifted her eyes to Heath's. It was no mystery about what lurked inside. An engagement ring. And she was in no hurry to see it.

In fact, she'd far rather Heath opened the box, took the ring and slid it onto her finger. That way it would be a fait accompli. She could convince herself that he'd simply swept her along, and keep telling herself that Heath was running her life for her—and keep resenting him for it.

Amy read the challenge in his eyes…and knew that he'd anticipated her. Heath wanted her to take the ring out of the box and put it on her own finger. She'd said she would marry him; now he wanted her to prove her willingness. He'd brought her here to this elegant restaurant, thrown it at her that he expected their marriage to be a real one and now he was waiting for her to get cold feet.

Did he think she was going to run away?

She glanced down at her hand. The fingers were pale and

nicely tended, her nails polished. On her ring finger there already sat a ring—Roland's ring. A sparkling, flawless, colourless two-carat solitaire in a modern platinum setting, that he'd given her on her twenty-first birthday.

Biting the soft inside of her cheeks, she sneaked a look back at the ring box on the table.

If she was going to marry Heath, she needed to wear the darn ring that lay in that little black box. With a deep breath she reached out and picked it up. The black velvet was soft under her fingers. She hesitated a moment, then lifted the lid with a burst of apprehension.

Her chest constricted. The ring that glowed against the luminescent white satin could only have been chosen for her.

A magnificent, old-fashioned, heart-cut golden diamond gleamed against white gold, surrounded by a row of smaller diamonds. The delicate filigree detail of the setting was astonishing. It didn't look like a modern knockoff. Her gaze flickered to Heath.

"This is Victorian."

"Yes." His gaze gave nothing away. "The colour matches your eyes."

She loved it. She didn't even want to think what it must've cost as she fondled it. Beneath her heart a peculiar hollowness filled her. Could Heath have chosen it by chance? Unlikely. Was she an open book to him? Could he read her at a glance? Unease stirred at that unbearable thought.

No, most likely Megan had picked it out. His sister had a stunning sense of style, and Megan knew of her love affair with Victorian jewellery. She'd often wondered if Megan had been responsible for choosing her favourite gift from Roland, the golden heart-shaped locket she loved so much. Her attention dropped back to the ring. With a note of longing she said, "It's so beautiful."

"I'm glad you like it."

Carefully she lifted it out of the box.

"You'll need to take that off." He pointed at Roland's solitaire. And started to reach for her hand.

"No!" Amy snatched her hand away, knowing this was something she had to do by herself. Without Heath's help. A flash of the conversation she'd had with Heath at the masked ball the night of Roland's fatal accident came to her like a thunderbolt.

"You're making a mistake."

It hadn't been the first time Heath had said it, but as always she didn't want to listen—mostly because she was starting to have dreadful doubts about her approaching wedding. She'd twirled the solitaire around her finger. "You don't know what you're talking about," she told him defiantly, refusing to think about the rumours she'd heard recently that Roland had a lover. It hadn't been the first time there had been whispers, but it had been the first time that she had taken heed. The suspicion that she'd been deceiving herself that Roland loved her—and only her—had taken hold. The romance she'd dreamed of since she turned seventeen was beginning to crumble.

But once Heath had moved away that night, her bravado had withered and she'd cornered Roland, demanding to know if the rumours of a celebrity lover were true. Roland had tried to laugh away her fears. But she'd persevered, and delivered her ultimatum: if her fiancé couldn't be faithful, then she didn't want to marry him.

Unconsciously Amy dropped her hand into her lap and stroked her belly beneath the feminine dress, Heath's ring warm in her palm. She didn't show yet. But she knew about the life inside her—even if no one else could see it yet. This baby of shame that she'd conceived.

The baby…the reason for this marriage. "You didn't want me to marry Roland."

Heath shrugged. "I didn't think he'd make you happy. You

ignored my warnings. And if Roland was what you wanted, then what was left for me to say?"

Amy stared at Heath. She'd had second thoughts, but she wasn't telling Heath. Not after that careless shrug. And certainly not when it might lead to too many other questions.

Defiantly, she held his gaze. "Roland was what I'd wanted since I turned seventeen."

Wanted…the word mocked her.

What had she known of wanting at seventeen? Everything she'd learned about wanting had been learned one fateful night.

Moonlight spilled in through the French doors, kissing his cheekbones, softening his wicked mouth and casting silver light over his naked shoulders. A memory of a hand stroking her hair off her face…of lips touching hers, tracing downward.

Just thinking of that night was enough to cause her body to catch fire. No, she didn't need that kind of wanting, the blazing passion she'd discovered burned inside her. *Never again.* It had been so intense, terrifying, she'd lost all sense of self. She'd done things, experienced things, she'd never dreamed of doing…of wanting. And in the process she'd awakened a passion she never wanted to experience again.

Could she marry Heath and keep her private heart untouched?

The marriage to Heath would be real. Sensual. That was clear. Would she be able to keep secret that wild, wanton side of herself she'd discovered the night her baby had been conceived? Hurriedly, she dropped the ring back into the box.

Turmoil raged through her.

Get a grip, she told herself fiercely. This was Heath. He'd offered to marry her for the baby's sake. For his family's sake. He'd never wanted marriage—clearly he didn't see himself as capable of falling in love. Knowing all that, it should be easy to restrain herself. Especially since she was pregnant, which would surely put the brakes on that unwelcome, passionate part of her.

She had her baby to think about now.

"I need to get back to work," said Amy, desperate to escape her thoughts—and this conversation.

"Oh no, you don't." His eyes glinted with annoyance. "I'm busy asking you to marry me and you still haven't put my ring on your finger."

Finally, she said, "It's funny isn't it? Ever since I was a little girl and first read fairy tales I've dreamed of a handsome guy and my wedding day—of the proposal and the ring and all the romance that went with the love and white lace." Amy pushed back her chair and the soft folds of the dress fell around her legs. "But now the stardust has been knocked out my eyes and I'm coming to realise that reality is nothing like that. It's about practicalities like an unmarried pregnancy…and making sure I still have a job."

"Forget about your damned job for today." As Heath shoved his coffee cup aside and rose to his feet, Amy realised again how big he was. "My mother is looking after reception. We might not have the romance you've always craved, but we've got today to get to know each other—and we're going to use every minute."

Heath hurried Amy along Marine Parade, oblivious to the crash of the surf to their left and the pale gold sunshine beating down on the sidewalk. His jacket hung from one finger over his shoulder, but his nonchalant manner was all fake. Inside his chest, his heart hammered and his jaw was set until it hurt, while his free hand clenched the ring box in his pocket.

All he was aware of was the woman who barely came up to his chin, but who filled such a huge space in his life.

A sideways glance revealed that she was chewing her lip in that way that she did when something was worrying her.

She was thinking too much. That wouldn't help right now. The velvet rubbed against his fingers. The bloody ring shouldn't still be in the box—it was supposed to be on her finger. He couldn't afford for her to have second thoughts.

Not now.

"Amy—"

"Oh, look." She'd stopped. Ahead of them a dark-haired toddler dressed all in pink had dropped a packet of toffees on the walkway. The little girl's face screwed up and she started to cry. Her harassed mother was trying to hold a grizzling baby, and bend to pick up the little girl's spilled candy at the same time.

Amy hurried forward. "Let me help."

The young mother threw her a grateful smile as the little girl stopped crying, her eyes fixed on Amy's pretty pink dress.

Let me help. With a wry smile, Heath shook his head and followed. It was such a typical Amy response. In a couple of efficient movements, she had the toffees back in the bag and the toddler's tears had vanished.

"Thank you."

"No worries," Amy gave the woman one of her sweet smiles—the kind of smile he'd kill dragons to receive.

Shadows flickered over Amy's expressive features as the trio made their way back to an abandoned pram, the baby settled on the mother's hip and the little girl clutching her mother's hand. Heath could've sworn Amy watched with something curiously akin to longing. A wave of tenderness swept over him.

Was she thinking about her baby?

"Come." He pulled the hand out his pocket and placed it under her elbow. "We're going to the aquarium."

"The aquarium?" She met his gaze blankly.

"Do you realise I don't even know what your favourite fish species is?" Heath looked at her in amusement as her mouth dropped open. "Or whether you're scared of sharks?"

"You need to know that?"

He nodded. "Without a doubt."

"It's been years since I've been to the aquarium," she said in bemusement.

"All the more reason to go." He linked his fingers through hers and led her toward the entrance. "Come on, Goody-Two-Shoes. Forget about work and other responsible things—have some fun."

She started to laugh, and Heath realised that he'd heard that sound far too rarely in past months.

"Goody-Two-Shoes?" she said after he'd paid the cashier. "Do you know how much I hated being called that?"

"Why? Did you yearn to be one of the Beaut-Bod Babes?" He shot her a wicked glance. "They'd never have worn pretty pink dresses and Victorian jewellery." He let his gaze linger appreciatively on her until her cheeks turned crimson.

"They were into leather and black lace," she sputtered. "Poseurs."

"Didn't stop every guy in the school from hitting on them." Heath couldn't help grinning.

"Even you," she said with a touch of acid, "although you should have known better."

He laughed until his ribs hurt.

They wandered through the glass tunnel past the pania reef tank. Unable to resist, Heath said with sly humour, "Those girls were man-eating sharks. And I only ever dated one of them."

"The pretty petite brunette." Amy rolled her eyes. "Easy to guess."

The conversation was heading for dangerous waters, so he fell silent and feigned a fascination with a mean-eyed shark, swimming lazily past behind the glass wall.

A little further on he pointed out a stingray to Amy and for the next twenty minutes contented himself with watching her wide-eyed enthusiasm. The sea horses were her favourites.

"They're so graceful," she told him.

Heath could've told her that she shared that trait. But he

didn't. Instead, he followed her upstairs to where a crocodile skulked in the bottom of a pool of water.

"Look at those teeth!"

Heath chuckled at the note of fascinated revulsion in her voice.

She peeked sideways. "He reminds me of you."

"Me?" Heath gave her a mock glare. "He's downright ugly."

"Okay, so you're not ugly." Colour rose in her cheeks as his eyebrows shot up. Hurriedly she glanced away. "But you both share a terrible reputation."

"Forget about my reputation," he advised, trying to suppress his irritation. "I've reformed."

"You'd better have."

"Anyway, crocodiles make great parents. I seem to remember they help their babies to hatch by tenderly rolling the eggs in between those evil-looking teeth." He gave the crocodile an old-fashioned look. "And don't the females put their babies in their mouths if there's danger nearby?"

Instead of smiling, Amy looked quite terrified. "It's starting to sink in," Amy said in a small voice, "that in a few months I'll have a baby, too. Hope I'll do as well as that armour-plated monster."

"You'll be a wonderful mother."

"Do you think so?" The amber eyes that met his were full of doubt.

"No doubt about it." Amy had been made for motherhood. Heath knew she'd take it very seriously—as she did everything she cared about.

"I've started to worry about that…" Her voice trailed away.

Heath slowed his steps and scanned her face. "Why? There's nothing to worry about. Take it from me, that's going to be one lucky kid."

"I wasn't sure that I'd be able to be everything that the baby needed."

"But you won't have to be." Heath drew the ring box back out his pocket and flipped it open. "I'll be there, too. Or had you forgotten?"

The hunch of her shoulders revealed her tension as she stared down at the ring. From this angle Heath couldn't see her face. A nasty sensation filled him. Was Amy considering reneging on their deal?

His head started to pound again. He wouldn't let her. Not after coming so far.

Slow down, he warned himself. *Don't frighten her off.*

"We need to talk." He shepherded her toward a seating area and waited for her to settle herself. Dropping his jacket next to her, he chose his words with care. "I'm not going to make you marry me."

She glanced away from the ring box in his hand and tilted her face up to him. The reflected light turned her amber eyes to a dull gold. "What do you mean?"

"This has to be your decision, Amy. I can't make it for you."

For a moment utter stillness surrounded her. "Are you suggesting that I actually *want* you to run my life?"

Maybe. But he had the sense not to say it as her face tightened. Amy gave off mixed signals. A mutinous expression was far preferable to the flare of resentment that he'd seen in her eyes after he'd bought her father's vineyard. To be honest he hadn't been prepared for that—she'd always seemed to appreciate Roland taking charge of their relationship. For Roland she'd always been sweet and biddable. Yet she slapped him down every time he tried to do anything for her. The difference must lie in the fact that she'd loved Roland…

She certainly didn't love him.

But Heath couldn't deny that he relished putting a spark in her eyes. He enjoyed riling her, causing her cheeks to flame with colour, so that she looked a world away from the goody-two-shoes that everyone called her.

But more than anything else in the world he wanted her to be happy. And right now she looked anything but.

He snapped the box shut. "I'm not going to force you to wear this ring. If you can't even put it on, then maybe it's not me that this marriage is a problem for—it's you."

Heath hadn't expected the blind panic that turned her eyes opaque.

"No, no, I ha—want to marry you." But before he could react to the joy that seared him, she glanced away. "It just that—"

She dropped her head into her hands. His brother's engagement ring scintillated in the iridescent light that glimmered through the aquarium. The ring she didn't want to take off— the bond she didn't want to break.

Something twisted deep inside him, putting a damper on his joy. Something dark and ugly and far too close to jealousy for his peace of mind. How low had he sunk to envy his dead brother and covet his fiancée?

Through her fingers, she whispered, "Damn, but I've made such a mess of this."

Heath did a double take. Amy never cussed. Never. A sudden burst of panic shook him. Had he pushed her too hard? He sank down beside her. "Tell me what you want me to do, Amy. And I'll do it."

Even if it meant compromising his own hopes of happiness for a future that stretched endlessly in front of him.

Her hands dropped from her face. "Will you?"

Did she have to ask? He took in the wide eyes, the quivering mouth. To be fair, she'd never known that he'd walk over burning coals for her. The seething depths of his emotions were something that he took great pains to hide from her.

"Within reason."

She held her hand out. "Put your ring on my finger, then."

The diamond already on her finger transfixed him. He couldn't bring himself to take his brother's ring off her finger.

Anything but that. Taking her engagement ring off, letting Roland go, was something she had to do herself.

He sucked a deep breath into his lungs. "First, you need to take off Roland's ring."

"I can't," she said, a suspicious glimmer of moisture silvering her eyes.

Bloody hell. This was not going to work. How could he have ever have thought there was a chance? The ghost of Roland would forever stand between them. Amy had loved his brother with her whole sweet heart. A wave of guilt flooded Heath that he was forcing her to take Roland's ring off her finger.

He deserved to be shot.

Disgusted with himself, Heath pushed himself to his feet. Letting the ring box fall into her lap, he muttered. "Forget it. Forget the whole damned thing."

"What are you—"

"This isn't going to work." He swung to face her, his hands balled in his pockets as regret washed through him.

"You don't want to marry me any longer?"

She looked unexpectedly devastated. Her bewildered expression rocked him. He gave a wretched sigh. "Hell, Amy, it's not that I don't want to marry you. It's just that—" *Roland.* Her love for Roland would always lie between them.

Amy bent her head and her graceful fingers played with the box lying in the folds of pink fabric of her dress. "What about the ring?" There was panic in her voice.

Heath resisted the impulse to step closer, to urge her, to beg her to take Roland's ring off…and open the box and put his ring where he'd always wanted it.

Instead, he shrugged. "Keep it." He didn't care about the damn ring. "I chose it for you."

Her head snapped back. The shock in her eyes had intensified. "*You* chose it?"

"Yep—who else could've chosen it?"

"I don't know. Megan, maybe."

"Megan?" He knew he sounded astonished. "Why would I have my sister choose your ring?"

"Because she's got great taste." Amy spread her hands in a helpless gesture and the velvet box tumbled off her lap. "To save you the bother."

She didn't have a clue…

"I wanted something that would suit you." His voice gentled. Like Amy, the ring had to be unique. One of a kind. "It had to be something you would enjoy wearing." Heath decided he'd said enough. But before she could ponder on what he'd given away, he glanced at the Rolex watch on his wrist.

The afternoon was almost gone. Amy must be exhausted. He reached forward and picked up his jacket and slipped it on. "Come, I'll take you home."

"I don't believe this!" Amy was on her feet, her eyes spitting sparks. "At lunch, you told me that being married wouldn't be easy—that we both had to work at it. Only hours later, you're eager to take me home and walk out on me simply because I didn't rip Roland's ring off my finger." Her breath came in little ragged bursts that caused Heath to stop dead in his tracks. "If you've had second thoughts, at least be honest—just tell me."

Her ire caused his heart to lighten. "This is not easy for me, Amy. I've never been a quitter. But I've taken this as far as I can. Now the ball is in your court."

Her expression shifted between relief, bewilderment, and something curiously like apprehension. "Heath—"

A group of Japanese tourists bustled passed, giving them curious looks. When they'd gone, Amy grabbed Heath's arm. "I know you've said you never had any intention of marrying, Heath, that you proposed because of the baby, out of a sense of obligation. So I can understand if you feel trapped and if you want to—"

"Change my mind?" He gave her a hard look as he finished the sentence for her.

If she only knew…

"Well, maybe you should. I mean, I know you said you wouldn't but that doesn't mean that you can't." After that bit of garble, Amy was looking anywhere but at him.

Heath rather liked this deliciously flustered, at-a-loss-for-words Amy. But the time had arrived for some straight truths. Heath squared his shoulders. "If you can't even bring yourself to take Roland's ring off your finger, you're not ready for this. That's the reason I'm walking away—it's for your sake."

Her forehead puckered. "But I don't want you to go. I'd rather you married me." And then she spoilt it all by clapping her hand over her mouth and looking utterly horrified.

It didn't get any better.

"My baby's going to need a father. We agreed on that."

Heath let out his breath in a soft hiss. The baby. Of course. This wasn't about what Amy wanted. It was about what Amy thought was best. For her baby.

Amy was already tugging at her ring finger.

Heath watched in speechless disbelief as she shoved Roland's sparkling diamond into her purse.

She'd done it.

His legs felt unaccountably weak, as if he'd run a marathon. Suddenly, he had an overwhelming need to sit down. He ignored it and rocked back and forth on feet planted hip-width apart.

"There." Lifting her chin, she gave him a challenging stare and presented him with her bare hand. "Happy now?"

It started to sink in that Amy was determined to marry him. If the set expression on her face was anything to go by, she wasn't going to let him walk away.

He let out the breath he'd unconsciously been holding. "Not yet," he said hoarsely, not daring to consider whether what would make him happy was within his reach.

"Okay." She bent to pick up the ring box where it had fallen. The golden diamond winked in a ray of sunlight. Beautiful. Seductive. Perfect for her. Poised, holding it between her fingers, ready to slip on, Amy let out her breath and said, "Will this make you happy?"

"Give it to me." Heath discovered he didn't want her angry when she put his ring on her finger. To his surprise, this feisty Amy obeyed. "May I have your left hand… please?"

She held out her hand with a delicate grace that caused his chest to tighten. Taking her slim fingers between his broad calloused ones, Heath slid the ring onto her finger, slowly, with great ceremony. It fitted as if it had been made for her. Suppressing a sigh of immense relief, he bent his head and kissed the finger on which the ring rested, a sliver of gratitude slicing through his heart.

She could have made it so much more difficult. But, by taking his brother's ring off, she'd met him halfway. Roland's ring had formed an impenetrable barrier between them. He couldn't have removed it. There would have been too much baggage. But she had done it—and her action gave him hope that maybe this marriage would work. Hell, it would work. It *must* work.

Despite the warm day, her fingers were unexpectedly cool between his. Heath lowered his head and pressed another kiss to her soft skin, reluctant to release her hand. The pale fingers trembled slightly under his lips and Heath suppressed a surge of triumph.

She did want him.

Amy was every bit as aware of him as he was of her. He parted his lips against her skin, a hot lingering gesture. Above his head he heard her breath catch. Satisfaction warmed him.

There would be no problem with the physical side of their marriage.

"That finger is supposed to lead straight to the heart."

Her unsteady voice washed over him, and he raised his head to stare into eyes the colour of summer honey.

Refusing to think about the past, or the future, Heath focused on the tension that simmered between them. It had to count for something. She desired him. Relentlessly, he held her gaze. The instant the amber eyes melted, Heath knew what he was going to do. All the talk about sex and marriage and the path to her heart had been too much.

It needed only one small shift of his feet for him to reach her. Then Heath covered her mouth with his.

He heard—tasted—her gasp.

His tongue swirled past the soft barrier of her lips, filling her mouth. He claimed her mouth with a calm deliberation that almost went to hell.

Closing his eyes, Heath forced himself to focus on the moment, on each breath, on every sensation. She tasted faintly of chocolate and mint. The inside of her mouth was hot and sweet and a sharp stab of desire pierced him.

"No!"

The lips uttering the inexplicable refusal moved beneath his and her hands shoved at his shoulders. Shaking himself, to get hold of his reactions, Heath ended the kiss.

"This is a public place." She pulled away and stared up at him, her eyes stretched wide with shock…and something more. Her pink tongue slid over her bottom lip causing his stomach to clench. Heath ached to press his mouth against that moist, plump lower lip. But the uncertainty in her face held him back.

"That's the only reason you said no? Because it's a public place?" He could take care of that.

"And there are kids around."

"Not right now." That space surrounding them was empty. But that wasn't all that was worrying her. Heath sensed her hesitation. "What else?"

"Heath, I don't want this."

"This?" His brows drew together. The power of his passion made him impatient. He knew what wanting tasted like. And there was no doubt that Amy wanted him. "You don't want to kiss? Not even if we find somewhere more private…someplace with no kids?"

He knew he sounded disbelieving. But, hell, he hadn't been mistaken. Amy wanted him. And her need had awoken a driving hunger in him.

She gave a little nod. "That's right."

"You don't want to kiss, but earlier at lunch you agreed that you'd make love with me once we're married." Heath shook his head. It made no sense.

Amy looked wretched, trapped. She opened her mouth and closed it again. He waited, refusing to make this easier for her. This was her last chance. She had to make up her mind; once they were married there would be no going back.

"It's not that I don't want…" She stopped, flushing. "Okay, maybe it is. Heath, I don't *want* to feel like this." The jerky words sounded ripped from her.

And he finished the rest of the sentence silently. *I don't want to feel like this…about you.* A flash of pain sliced through him, followed by sympathy for her plight.

Guilt. It must be eating her alive.

And she was alive—very much so. Her response to him proved it. She hadn't—he prayed—buried her heart with his brother.

But guilt gnawed at him too. For a different reason. He felt bad because he was pretty pleased that she was confused— it meant that however much she'd loved Roland, at least she still wanted him, Heath, the bad boy she'd always given a wide berth. That meant that he wouldn't have an emotionless cardboard cutout in his bed. Heath didn't want a sacrifice in his bed; he wanted a flesh-and-blood wife.

"Don't worry about it," he said gruffly and shoved his hands into his pockets to stop himself from drawing her close. "Once we're married, everything will be easier."

She flicked him a little glance. "That's what I've been trying to tell myself, but I'm scared—"

"Scared?" He pounced on that. The last thing in the world Heath wanted was a terrified bride. "Of me? But why, for God's sake?"

Her straight white teeth closed on a bottom lip kissed to fullness. A fresh blast of want shook him. And shadows instantly flickered in her eyes.

"Not of you. Not really. I'm scared that if I let this happen…" Amy covered her face. "Oh, I can't tell you."

Heath frowned at her as he tried to work out what the hell was going on inside that feminine brain. This was about more than guilt.

But what?

"Amy." He withdrew both hands from his pockets and reached to cup her face between his hands and tilt it up. The eyes that met his were full of reluctance. Doing his best to look reassuring, he said, "Don't hold back. This is Heath, I've known you most of your life. There's nothing you can't tell me."

She gave a shattered sigh. "You're wrong. There's plenty that's impossible to tell you." Her gaze slid away, then returned a split second later. "As for knowing me…you don't know this me. I don't even know *this* side of me—it's embarrassing!"

Relief flooded him. Amy was talking about desire… about her ravenous response to his kiss, about wanting to make love with him.

The laugh that escaped him came from deep within his stomach. It was full of relief. His fingers slid along the silky skin beneath her jaw, under her ears, and cradled her nape.

"Believe me," he said huskily, "I very much want to get to know this side of you."

"Heath!"

Her scandalised whisper had him saying, "So we'd better get married quickly. Because, make no mistake, ours will not be a passionless marriage."

"You promised to give me time!"

The plea was accompanied by an apprehensive glance that Heath had no power to resist.

"Ah, Amy—" He reached for her.

"No!" Her lashes swept down before he could read what lay hidden there.

A flare of fear shot up his spine. But she didn't move away and Heath took heart from that fact, dismissing his fears as unfounded. She'd agreed to marry him. She'd removed Roland's ring. She wore his ring on her finger.

All that remained was to get the wedding arranged as quickly as possible. He'd involve his mother and his sister and get the ball rolling. Amy wasn't the kind of woman who would jilt a man. Her sense of right wouldn't allow it.

Nothing would go wrong.

His lips curved into a smile that was intended to reassure her. "And I will give you time. But make no mistake, we will be lovers. Don't think that this is going to be an empty shell of a marriage."

This time when he dipped his head, Heath was confident she knew what was coming. And that she would respond.

He was right. Her ribs rose and fell against his chest as her breathing grew shallow and she inched closer. Heath's hands closed around her waist. The filmy pink dress she wore presented no barrier. Her flesh was warm and soft under his fingers.

Need shook him.

This time there was no demur. She was ready for him, and her lips parted before he touched her.

This time his kiss was explicit, possessive, full of warning and dark desire. It was time for Amy to accept that she would be his woman—his wife—in every way.

Seven

The wedding date had been set for the coming Saturday.

Five days. That was all she had, Heath told Amy late on Monday afternoon as he leaned over the wooden counter above her desk, effectively cornering her. Most of the winery staff had already finished for the day. Amy was aware of the silence in the huge reception area…and that they were alone.

Despite the drumming of her pulse in her temples, she wanted to protest at the speed with which everything was happening. Kay had already been by to talk about the choice of food that the caterers would supply; less than an hour ago Alyssa had offered to call and invite everyone on the guest list that had been whipped up; and Megan had bombarded Amy with demands to go into town to choose a dress. The Saxon family had embraced the idea of her marrying Heath with wholehearted enthusiasm and everyone had flung themselves into rapidly putting together the wedding between her and Heath. And Amy found herself simply agreeing to everything.

Yet how could she object? Amy didn't dare risk Heath calling everything off. Not with the joy and hope that this hasty wedding had brought the Saxons. Not with Kay looking happier than she'd looked in a long time…her godmother had abandoned all talk of staying for a while with her family in Australia. The wedding—and the baby—had given Kay a new lease on life.

Now Amy gave Heath a glance from under her lashes as he towered over her. Understandably his features showed strain, his cheekbones spare, hardly the picture of the deliriously delighted groom.

No, Heath was doing the best he could. For her. For his family. For everyone.

There was another reason why a quickie wedding brought Amy relief. *The baby.* It wouldn't be long before she started to show. It might be cowardly, but Amy knew that she would be happier if she were married before that happened. Even though that meant all sorts of other endless complications. Like the fact that she'd be marrying Heath instead of Roland…and everyone would be speculating about which Saxon brother's baby she was carrying in her womb.

She rolled her chair back to put some distance between them and said, "I'll be glad when this hullabaloo is all over."

He didn't smile. If anything his eyes grew darker than ever. Devil's eyes. Yet he'd been so kind. This was no devil, this was Heath, and she'd known him all her life…

His eyes intent, he rested his folded arms on the top of the polished wooden counter and asked, "Where do you want to go afterwards?"

"Afterwards?"

"After the wedding. For a honeymoon."

Honeymoon? Liquid heat melted through the bottom of her stomach at the idea of going somewhere all alone with Heath. She had a vision of them sharing a candlelit dinner in velvety dusk. Just the two of them. She swallowed. "Uh…we don't need a honeymoon. No one will expect us to—"

"I think we need one." There was no room for negotiation in those five words. "It will do us good to have some time away to get to know each other."

Spend time alone with Heath? Even though she'd known him forever…being alone with him was something else.

Amy gulped in a mouthful of moist evening air, suddenly overwhelmingly conscious that they were the only people in the winery. The silence weighed heavily on her.

Her words came in a rush. "Heath, I know this isn't going to be a platonic marriage." He'd made that clear enough. "But we don't need a honeymoon. This isn't going to be that kind of marriage."

His eyes narrowed dangerously. "That kind of marriage?"

Amy's heart fluttered at the intensity in the dark depths.

"Uh…" She started to stammer. Blood rose in her cheeks. Her stomach plunged and a sense of her whole world shifting shook her. "I just meant that it's not a love match. No one's going to believe that. Not with Roland dead a little over two months."

A muscle moved in his jaw. "People will believe that grief brought us together."

She stared at him, her mouth dry, her throat suddenly tight. In that instant no one existed other than the two of them. "That's what you're going to tell everyone?"

"I won't need to tell them. That's what they'll assume. As long as you don't tell anyone anything to the contrary." He was frowning now.

"And what else are they going to assume?" she asked, because she had to, but shuddering inside, her every sensibility recoiling. Amy still didn't know how she was going to handle the speculation. "Everyone will be counting on their fingers, wondering if the baby is Roland's—" through her lashes she could see his jaw tightening "—or yours."

His features looked like rock. Hard. Implacable. "Everyone knows you have always loved Roland. There will be no reason to gossip about the baby's paternity."

Her lover moved, his body sliding over hers. A beam of moonlight revealed the stark lines of his face. A side of him she'd never seen. A moment of sanity—too brief—caused her to hesitate, then he kissed her, openmouthed, erotic kisses that turned her limbs to water and the moment passed. Never to return. With a sigh of delight she succumbed.

Staring into Heath's face, adrenalin surged through her. "What if they do?"

"No one will dare speculate."

The implacability in that hard face convinced her. Heath looked terrifying. And somewhere inside her, warmth stirred at his protectiveness. That warmth was worrying, too. What if she did something to make him think she wanted him? Because she did. Even though she wasn't ready to admit that yet. Not to herself...and certainly not to him.

All the more reason to stall a honeymoon.

"But what about the summer festival?" Amy scrambled around for excuses. "I'm supposed to be helping arrange that. Things are crazy around here right now." She grabbed a to do list off her desk and waved it in his face. "I can't just take off."

Nothing changed in his expression. "I think you can. It'll be our honeymoon. Everyone will understand."

Uh-huh. His face was filled with purpose. There was going to be no getting around this.

"How long?" Amy finally caved in.

"Five days—that will give you plenty of time to help with the festival when you get back. I'll help, too." His gaze raked her. "Better prepare me some to do lists, too."

That didn't reassure her one iota.

* * *

As the days hurtled past and the wedding day rushed closer, the tension within Amy rose to the breaking point. Her control over her own life was being eroded away. She'd had no say in the date of the wedding, or the decision to go on a honeymoon. She was starting to resent Heath's ruthless purposefulness…and beginning to feel increasingly pressured.

But there was one thing that was within her control…her decision to marry Heath—only she knew the real reason why she was doing it. She'd never believed that knowledge was power. And she knew she shouldn't be holding out on him. The guilt was killing her. Heath deserved to know.

She tried several times to talk to him—she really did—but every time, at the last minute, her courage gave out. Coward. But she promised herself that she wouldn't marry him—not without telling him what she found so hard to talk about.

But every day it became harder and harder to confront him. Until, on the eve of their wedding, all Amy's good intentions of telling Heath exactly why she was marrying him flew right out the window.

The evening started well enough. Heath had planned a dinner at Chosen Valley. Just her father and the two of them. It was a casual evening—no one dressed up; Amy wore a pair of jeans that had grown tight around her waist teamed with an Icebreaker top. Heath, as usual, wore his signature black jeans and T-shirt. But for once she saw past the bad boy wear.

His consideration had touched a chord deep within her that he'd known she would want to spend a last quiet evening with her father.

The meal was fantastic. Afterwards, all three of them moved to the sitting room, where dim sconces bathed the room in a soft glow. Josie, Heath's housekeeper, brought a cup of hot chocolate for Amy while the two men sampled a selection of ports. Much to Amy's embarrassment, her father had almost turned maudlin as he recounted tales of Amy's childhood and Heath let him ramble. In fact, apart from the odd, indecipherable glance, Heath appeared to have forgotten that she was there.

Finally, he seemed to recall her presence.

"Have you taken your iron and vitamins today, Amy? It's going to be a long day tomorrow. You'll need all the energy you can get."

All her resentment at his high-handedness coalesced. She forgot about what he'd done for her. Forgot about what he was doing for her baby.

"Stop telling me what to do!" Amy discovered she was breathing hard. "Despite what you might think, I'm no longer a child."

The words were overloud in the gracious room. She faced him, her heart pounding. Deep inside she knew she was being unfair. But she couldn't stop the childish resentment that overwhelmed her. Ever since he'd bought Chosen Valley, this had been simmering inside her.

"Calm down," said Heath.

"Then stop trying to take over my life." Amy felt like she was losing control of hers.

"Amy!" Her father's groan increased her remorse. "Heath saved me. Can't you understand that? I know you wanted to save us, Amy-girl—but it wouldn't have worked."

"What do you mean, Ralph?" Heath intervened quietly.

Ralph Wright looked at Amy, apology written over his still-handsome face. "I know you wanted to help, but I was in too deep. I left the harvest too late…the rains came—" he shook his head "—there was no other way."

"Dad, it's okay." Amy rested a hand on her father's shoulder, wishing desperately that her father had never started this conversation.

Heath's gaze settled on Amy and his voice gentled. "What were you planning?"

"I'd met with the bank…I tried to extend our credit. They weren't interested." The memory of her humiliation spread through her. "I'd planned to start a bed-and-breakfast venture. It was something I'd always dreamed about doing. I delivered a business plan."

"You should've told me."

As she held his gaze, she read his intention there. "What, so you would've bullied them into giving me a loan?"

He gave a slight smile. "You credit me with too much power. I couldn't have talked the bank into giving you a loan—but I might have been able to stand as guarantor for the loan. Or I'd have advanced you the money—"

"No." Amy shook her head. "That was the last thing I wanted."

"But why?"

How to explain? Reluctantly, she admitted, "I didn't want to feel indebted to you. I'm a grown-up, I didn't want you sorting out my problems as you always have." As he had when she'd been a schoolgirl. Except it hadn't stopped there. He'd bought her home. He'd arranged a position for her as PA at Saxon's Folly. She'd felt like a puppet on a string.

There was a strange expression on his face as he set down his port glass and said with fixed intensity, "Amy, I haven't thought of you as a child for years." Something about how he looked at her left her breathless. Before she could reply, he added, "You'd just started dating Roland back then. Did you turn down his offer of help, too?"

He hadn't offered. And she hadn't asked. In fact, she and Roland had argued about her plans. Careful to keep all expression from her voice, she said, "I discussed it with Roland. He travelled so much, he said that in the future I'd be going with him––he thought a bed-and-breakfast business would tie me down." They hadn't been engaged back then, but Amy had known Roland's intentions were serious. He'd known she was the marrying kind, and he hadn't wanted his wife to work. Period. He'd been with her father on that. A wife's position was to support her husband and make his life easier.

The plan she'd drafted for the bank had been filed away, and she'd shelved the dream. Roland had said that once they were married there would be enough to keep her busy helping him with the entertaining he did in his role as marketing manager.

She'd finally managed to convince Roland that while they were dating she needed an income, her independence. He hadn't liked it. But he'd gone along with her working at Saxon's Folly. She'd turned down his offer of an allowance—worried that it came with strings attached. Amy had wanted her white wedding to be exactly that.

She touched her belly where her baby lay.

Her pure, white wedding was yet another dream that had been shattered. After all those years she'd spent refraining from intimacy before marriage, wanting to keep herself pure for her husband—her wedding gift of love—she'd lost even that.

A memory of a mouth against her neck, of hot words whispered in her ear caused a frisson to run through her.

Amy shivered with delight as his very male fingers lingered against her bare skin that glowed like white rose petals in the moonlight. It was wrong, this ecstasy, so very wrong. But she couldn't bring herself to tell him to stop. The burning, the hunger, that his touch had ignited consumed her.

Now, in the presence of her father and husband-to-be, she ruthlessly suppressed the wanton images. She should never have given in to the temptation. She'd broken her chastity pledge to herself. She was as bad as Roland.

During the two years they'd dated, and the year they'd been engaged, she'd never considered that Roland might be unfaithful. That had been part of her vision of true love. She'd believed they would spend that time getting to know each other—building a delicious romance between them.

But Roland hadn't shared her beliefs.

When she'd confronted him about the rumours of another woman, and issued her ultimatum, Roland had blamed her unrealistic chastity vow. He'd argued that if she'd slept with him rather than insisting on an archaic white wedding and a virginal wedding night, he wouldn't have needed to stray. He'd made her doubt her values—her beliefs—that night. She'd felt pressured, upset. She'd started to believe it was *her* fault that he slept around with other women—that it was *her* fault that he'd been less than faithful to her.

It had made her doubt everything.

Her feelings. Her values. Even who she was. Her head had been a mess.

And now Heath was watching her every move, as if he were trying to see inside her head. Amy flushed. And found she had to glance away. Before he read exactly what she was thinking.

The darkness hid the hectic colour that his caresses had seared her skin in a hot flood. A dreamy lassitude assailed her. She could pretend this was a beautiful dream, that the nightmare world of earlier tonight had vanished forever. That she'd waken in the morning in her beloved's arms and everything would be right...

Avoiding Heath's gaze, Amy told herself that Heath couldn't possibly know what she was thinking.

Heath stared hungrily at the high colour that stained Amy's cheeks. She wouldn't meet his eyes.

Did she know that he wanted to kiss her, taste her lips, leave them coloured with the same rosy flush that suffused her cheeks? She had a ripeness to her that suited her. Even in casual wear, she managed to look sultry. So sexy. So incredibly tempting. Nothing like the good girl that everyone thought her to be.

And his secret knowledge left him wanting her more than ever.

Ralph had moved onto everyday talk about rain and weather forecasts and Heath heard himself reply, even though all his attention was focused on Amy. Only Amy. At last she turned her head and glared at him, telling him without words that she knew exactly what he was thinking. Heath suppressed the wild, joyous grin that almost spread over his face.

Sweet, innocent Amy.

If only it was that easy…

It would take a lot more than a glare to stop what he was feeling right now. He'd always wanted her with this ache that never left. She pursed her mouth in that delightfully disapproving way that made him want to kiss her until that tight pink rosebud mouth blossomed under his. He winked at her. She glared harder, no hint of amusement in her eyes.

Maybe he wasn't playing fair. He stretched his legs, wishing he could whisper at her not to worry, it would be okay. He'd promised not to pressure her.

Ralph was looking at him, too. Heath felt himself flush at being caught staring like a lovestruck idiot at the man's daughter.

"Are you ready?" Ralph asked.

Heath blinked. Ready? Hell, yes. He gave his father-in-law a reckless smile. He'd been ready years ago. "Yes, I'm ready for tomorrow."

Lifting the small glass of ruby-coloured port, Heath took a sip of the rich sweet liquid. He couldn't believe that it had gotten this far, that Amy was finally going to marry him tomorrow. Euphoria rushed through him.

"I never dreamed that Amy might one day marry you," Ralph said with a fond glance at his daughter, who was cupping her mug of chocolate between her palms. "Can't think why I never thought of it before. It makes sense. You two fit well together."

"I was engaged to Roland," Amy said, setting down the mug with a clatter.

"I think Heath will be better for you."

"Why do you say that, Daddy?"

Heath tilted his head back against the top of the chair, confident that his emotional response to Amy was his closely guarded secret, but more than a little interested in his future father-in-law's take on the situation.

The older man swirled the dark port around his glass and took a sip. "Just that you've always been a homebody and Roland was never here. He was always off gallivanting."

"But that was his job," Amy protested. "I accepted that. He'd even told me that after we were married he wanted me to go with him, help him entertain."

Her father shook his head. "It was more than that. Roland was restless...never satisfied. You would've hated being dragged around in his wake."

Ralph was more perceptive than he'd dreamed, Heath realised. He'd had Roland pegged. His adoptive brother had always been a rover—with a roving eye to match. Not that Amy knew about that.

"You think he would've found me unsatisfying? That I would've bored him?" Amy's eyes flashed at her father, and Heath suppressed a smile at the ridiculousness of the question.

"Amy-girl, it's not a criticism of you...it's the kind of man he was. Wild. Restless."

Amy gave a little laugh, but her fingers played with the folded linen napkin. "You're confused, Daddy. Wild and restless describes Heath exactly. Look at him."

The inspection that Ralph gave him through narrowed eyes didn't miss a thing. Not the monochrome black shirt and jeans, not the strain around his mouth. Suddenly, Heath was sure that his future father-in-law had seen more than Heath wanted. Tensely, he waited for Ralph's assessment.

But all Ralph said was, "I don't know about that, my girl. Never believed all that rubbish myself. Heath has always been where he's been needed, always worked hard, he's always there." He set his glass down. "But it's not for a father to tell his daughter about the man she's marrying."

Slowly, Heath let out the breath that he'd been holding. His secret was safe. But the knowledge that someone had questioned the acts he'd been blamed for, warmed him.

"What do you mean?" Amy was asking her father.

Ralph gave Heath a conspiratorial smile. "I've said enough. It's time for me to leave."

That smile told Heath everything he needed to know. Ralph was not going to say more. Relaxing a little, Heath pushed his chair back and rose to his feet.

Amy came with him to the door to see her father out, but Heath saw that she had no intention of leaving. Her hands clenched and unclenched, revealing her inner tension. She looked like a woman with a lot on her mind.

After Ralph had driven off, Heath rested a courteous arm around her waist and ushered her to the sitting room.

"You're upset."

She shrugged his arm off. "A little." Amy opened the glass doors and stepped out onto the wooden deck.

Flipping the verandah lights on, Heath followed more slowly. Outside the night was warm, and the air held a tang of salt from the distant ocean. The light from the full moon spilled across the landscape, giving it an eerie, fairy-world quality.

"Are you angry with me?" Heath wanted to get a clear handle on her state of mind, so that he could assess what needed to be said.

She turned to face him, her arms wrapped around her middle. "I'm angrier with myself."

Heath started to smile. "Why?"

"Because I'm a coward."

He did laugh then. But she gave him a reproachful look that told him this was no laughing matter. Heath restrained himself with difficulty. Anyone who knew Amy knew that she never shied away from doing what was right. If something needed telling, she could be trusted to say it.

"I wouldn't let it worry you."

"But it does." Her bottom lip jutted out and he longed to kiss it, take it between his teeth and play with it. Perhaps not quite yet. Soon…

His gaze lifted and in the harsh moonlight he met the rebellious golden eyes. The laughter left him. Instantly, his body hardened. One glance. That was all it took.

He drew a steadying breath, controlled the rush of emotion and centred his attention on the discussion they were having. No mean feat. "It's not just yourself you're angry with. You're a little mad at me, too. Right?"

She didn't reply.

Heath stepped closer and ventured into forbidden territory. "Because I'm alive and Roland isn't?"

Her eyes stretched wide with shock. "No! Never that."

Heath's breath escaped in a slow hiss. There was no reason to feel guilty for the deep emotion she stirred in him. His brother was dead. Amy was his.

Even though she didn't love him.

She would learn to love him. Heath wasn't conceited but he knew women cast him little glances all the time—imagining his prowess as a lover, measuring his strength as a man, his excellence as a provider.

After the wedding tomorrow, they would have all the time in the world, starting with their honeymoon. She would learn to love him. *She had to.*

Thinking about her claim earlier that he was both wild and

restless, he asked, "Why do you persist in thinking I'm still the wild, restless teenage boy? Does it make it easier?"

"What do you mean?" But her rapid prevarication and the flash of vulnerability in her eyes told him she knew exactly what he meant.

"I suspect it's because that way you can tell yourself that I'm the bad boy—that I've got nothing in common with you, the good girl."

"That's not true. I don't think that." But her eyes slid away from his. After a moment she looked back at him. "But you did some wild things when you were young."

"Some," he conceded. "But not as many as everyone blamed me for."

"But those that you did were awful."

"Not all were my deeds. Sometimes I just copped the blame."

Uncertainty flickered in her eyes. "Is that true?"

"Sure."

"So who did you cop the blame for?"

He shrugged. "That's a no-brainer. And it's ancient history."

"Who?"

"My brothers. Their friends."

"They wouldn't have done that."

He laughed at her naiveté. "They were boys. I was the youngest. It's perfectly normal. And sometimes I even liked copping the blame. It made people forget I was the baby."

"Megan was the baby."

"Yes, but she was a girl."

Amy rolled her eyes. "Oh, good grief!"

"You still talked to me in those days." He could remember one incident clearly.

"I knew my mother would've wanted me to be your friend." Her arms unfolded and dropped away as her eyes grew dreamy with long-ago memories.

Amy had always been aware of the right thing to do. Yet

her friendship had ignited his awareness of the girl with grave golden eyes and her prim rosebud mouth. He remembered the day that he'd first noticed the curve of her breasts under a snug white singlet and how it had affected him. He could remember wanting to kiss her…but deciding she was still a kid.

He could wait.

The bad boy and the good girl. They'd grown up on neighbouring vineyards; she was the daughter of one of his mother's best friends.

And they'd been friends.

Almost.

Until she'd turned sixteen and it had become apparent that she idolized Roland, and he'd started to put space between them.

Roland. Always Roland. And now she was pregnant with Roland's baby. The swollen mounds of her breasts pulled the T-shirt tight and announced her fertile condition quite clearly. But some things never changed. He still couldn't keep his eyes off her.

"I think she'd be happy."

"Who?" He'd lost track of the conversation. Heath looked guiltily away from her lush shape.

"My mother." A little crinkle formed between her eyes as she gave him a puzzled stare. "I always knew she'd be happy I married one of Kay's boys."

"Is that why you decided you were in love with Roland?" Incredulity hardened his voice. "Because you thought your mother would've wanted it?"

She hesitated. "Don't be silly. I'd never have married Roland for that reason."

But Heath wasn't so certain. She must've missed her mother dreadfully. An only child. Kay's goddaughter. "Are you sure?"

"Yes! Of course, I'm sure."

"Ever thought that you could've decided that it was me you loved not Roland?"

"Heath!" She gave a little laugh. "But it was Roland."

"Why? What made him so special?"

"I don't know…" She lifted her shoulders. "But when I opened his present on my seventeenth birthday, I knew…" Her voice trailed away.

A pang of dismay pierced right through him. "Knew what?"

"That he was the one. He gave me this." Her fingertips brushed the locket. "It was so romantic, so perfect."

The gold heart could've been made for Amy. He'd known the moment he'd laid eyes on it. Just as he'd known the ring would be right. The smile he gave her was barbed. "So if I'd given you a romantic Victorian locket studded with diamonds, would you have decided I was the one?"

Her eyes studied him in puzzlement. "It wasn't about the gold or diamonds."

"I know. It was about connecting with what you liked."

"Yes." Her eyes flickered. "And you didn't."

"No, you're right, I didn't. But you're marrying me, and my mother is certainly happy enough about that." He gave her a smile. But he found he couldn't let it go. Stretching forward, he placed a hand on her stomach, felt her start. "Just think, it could have been my child."

For a moment she looked at him and time seemed to stand still. Shadows shifted in the golden eyes. She licked her bottom lip nervously and started to say something.

The sight of that slick bottom lip caused his stomach to tighten. All the desire he'd felt over the years, pooled between his thighs. Reckless with want, he said, "God, I can't wait to make you mine."

"You promised me time." Her expression shifted, her eyes growing blank in the moonlight. She crossed her arms over her breasts. "It's getting cold out here. Time to go in."

Heath hadn't noticed a difference in the temperature. He tipped his head sideways. "There's no wind."

"Well, then, maybe it's just me. I'm cold."

He couldn't stop thinking about how she would feel in his arms. He needed to hold her, touch her, make sure this was real. Perhaps he was being too optimistic. Perhaps her love for his brother would always be a wall between them and she might never learn to love him.

But it was worth taking a chance.

Eyes filled with determined purpose, he moved to her. "Then let me warm you up."

Eight

"Oh, God!"

He hadn't warmed her, he'd set her on fire. Amy's fingers touched her lips. They felt swollen where Heath had just kissed her with pulverising thoroughness. Sensitive. Tingling. She lifted her lashes to find Heath watching her through narrowed eyes that did nothing to stem the turbulence…the aching…that rolled within her. She despised herself for it.

"Amy, don't."

He must have read her self-loathing in her eyes. He stood there, strong, magnificent, his eyes full of an emotion that she didn't recognise. Pain? Passion? She didn't know any more. He confused her so. She confused herself. As for the feelings he aroused in her…

"Amy, don't look like that."

But even as he reached for her, she shut her eyes to block out the sight of him. Amy folded her arms tightly around herself to fend him off.

How could she be feeling like this? It made no sense. Yet she couldn't stop thinking about how his lips had moved on hers, how her heart had jumped and twisted over as desire flashed through her. For one blinding instant it had felt utterly, heart-stoppingly fabulous.

Until reality had set in and she'd remembered…this was Heath.

"I'm sorry. I promised you time." His voice was low, repentant. This time the arms that came around her were gentle as he pulled her to rest against the vibrant heat of his body. Amy tried to resist. But it was unexpectedly good to be in his arms. In the coolness of the moonlit night, his flesh was warm against her, his heartbeat solid. Instantly, her body was on fire, even though she knew that he had no intention of kissing her again, that this time he was offering nothing but comfort.

He'd comforted her before…and where had that ended?

In desperation Amy shut the little voice out and let her hands creep up his chest. His T-shirt was soft under her fingertips and his chest lifted under her palms as he sucked in a deep, shaking breath. Good. At least she knew that he wasn't finding this easy…that he couldn't just switch on and switch off like a robot. It made her feel a little better, a little stronger to know that this…this…wildness wasn't confined to her alone.

There was a certain insanity in what she did next. Afterwards she told herself she'd been testing him…trying to see if he was as in control as he always seemed. If she was the only one being jerked about like a puppet on a string. Linking her fingertips around his neck, Amy followed her mad instincts. Just then, tipping back her head, planting a kiss on his jaw seemed like the right thing to do.

But it didn't stop there.

The night was filled with the sound of denim rubbing against denim as he stepped closer and yanked her to him. She gasped. And Heath gave a deep moan that shook his tall frame and his mouth took hers in a kiss that made her knees go weak.

His mouth ravaged hers. His hunger ignited her own unruly desire. She squeezed her eyes more tightly shut and allowed herself to be towed along by the uncontrollable force, her hands clinging to his neck.

By the time he lifted his head, Heath was panting. As Amy cracked her eyes open she caught a glint of triumph, too.

Despair set in.

It was always going to be like this.

He'd kiss her, caress her, send her up in flames, and she'd lose all willpower. And, even worse, now he knew that she was vulnerable.

She simply couldn't understand what was happening to her. It wasn't as if she loved Heath. She'd loved Roland. How could she lust after Heath like…like a bitch in heat? The image didn't sit well with Amy. It didn't fit with the person she'd always considered herself to be. Whatever he said, Heath was a wild one. He didn't even believe in marriage… why should he, when he could have countless brief affairs? Heck, he'd told her himself that he'd never even *wanted* to marry.

How could she let herself sink to such depths where she became one of a legion of many? Where was her self-respect? Why did he have this horrible power over her body? How could she go against everything she believed in about love…about marriage just for the sake of this overpowering carnal hunger?

Feeling sick and utterly disgusted with herself, Amy wrenched herself out of his arms. The desperate need to escape him forced the words out of her, "*I can't do this.* I can't marry you."

He grabbed her as she rushed past. "It's too late to pull out, Amy."

Terrified that he'd kiss her again—or cradle her against his heart—she broke out of his grip, her breathing ragged. "It would be wrong for me to marry you."

"You're going to jilt me, then?" The dark eyes glittered in the reflected light that spilled from the house, revealing a wariness that made her want to weep.

Steadying herself against the doorframe, Amy hauled in a deep breath. "We can call everyone now…tonight…let them know that there won't be a wedding." The words tumbled over each other. "That way no one will be jilted."

"But I haven't decided to call it off." He said it so softly that for a long simmering second Amy thought she'd misheard.

"*We have to*. Heath, I can't—"

"Why?" he interrupted her, his voice harsh in the night. "Answer me that one question, Amy. Why don't you want to marry me?"

She barely understood herself. All she knew was that she feared the wild passion he aroused within her. Grasping at straws, she said, "You don't even believe in marriage."

"How can that be true? I'm marrying you, aren't I?" he said with incontrovertible logic.

Only out of a sense of family obligation. "But you don't believe in love," she flung at him.

"That's it?" The tension in his face eased and he took half a step toward her. "That's the only reason you won't marry me?"

Amy recoiled. "I don't love you, either. Marriage vows should be sacred. I can't lie in a church. Vowing to love, honour and obey you will be a lie. Don't ask me to do it." It would haunt her for the rest of her life.

Heath froze and his mouth twisted. "Then we'll get married on the beach."

"Don't be facetious!"

"I'm not going to let you back out of this—"

"I'm not going to vow to love you. You can't want me to marry you," she interrupted, "not if I don't want to."

"Oh, yes I can." His gaze scorched her, leaving her feeling branded. "There are good reasons for this wedding. Reasons better than love. You're pregnant. Our families are close—our mothers were best friends. You get to return to your family home."

Amy had to admit that it was a formidable list of reasons why this marriage would be a good one. But it wasn't enough. Not any more. Not without telling him the truth. "I can't—"

"I'm sick of hearing that you can't!"

His eyes snapped in the silver light, his body coiled and tense. Amy could sense the frustration and rage radiating from him as he said, "It's too late. You can't *not* marry me. My parents are happier than they've been in months. You will marry me in the morning. Because my parents want it."

A rush of her own anger filled her at his hardheadedness. "Well, go to the church tomorrow and wait. You can't force me to show up." She turned away, ready to leave. Inside she was trembling from the bitter exchange.

She hadn't wanted this.

From behind her he murmured, "If you don't arrive tomorrow, Amy. Then I will leave Saxon's Folly."

Shock made her freeze. But she didn't turn around. "What do you mean?"

"I will be winemaker of Chosen Valley and I will never again bring in a harvest at Saxon's Folly."

At that she spun around and she met his relentless, flat, black gaze. "You can't do that to me."

"Try me." Heath spoke through lips that barely moved.

Panic flooded Amy. She sensed that he would not back down. "You'd force me to marry you—even though you said it had to be my decision?"

He hesitated. For an instant she thought he was going to soften his stance, then his shoulders squared. "Yes, I would. It's too late to have second thoughts now, Amy."

Forcing herself to ignore the pulse drumming in her head, she scanned his face, taking in every stony feature. He would do it. And Amy knew that it would forever drive a wedge between him and his father. She couldn't bear for that to happen. She couldn't bear to know that she might have prevented it.

Would it be such a hardship to be married to Heath? Amy placed her shaking fingers against her temples, struggling to think clearly. What she decided now would shape the rest of her life—and Heath's…and his parents' lives, too.

Her instincts urged her to run as far away from him as she could. The powerful emotions he aroused in her terrified her. Could she give herself up to such a crazy passion? Could she marry a man who'd been a serial dater? A man incapable of committing himself to loving one woman?

Heck, it wasn't as if she was in danger of falling in love with him.

So why was she making it into such a big deal? Heath never intended to marry anyone; it wasn't as though she was ruining his chance at finding true love.

And she'd forgotten the reason for marrying him in the first place.

Her baby.

Their baby.

The baby needed a father. And who better to marry than the baby's real father?

"We'll be married tomorrow." Her baby's father spoke from behind her rigid back. Not soft words of comfort. Or whispers of desire. These words were ice-edged, as hard as the man himself. "There will be no more doubts. Understood?"

A swift glance at Heath's face had her quaking in trepidation. Her throat was too tight to reply, so she nodded slowly.

But even that didn't soften the frown that darkened his face.

She couldn't tell him the truth tonight. He was so angry. And she was too mad at him to make sense tonight. It wasn't the right time. It would lead to recriminations…bitter words better left unsaid. It would have to wait.

Until they were married.

Amy knew she had no choice but to marry him. Heath was right. Their baby was going to draw a splintered family together.

But she wished it could've been different. Her shoulders slumped. "I really despise you, Heath Saxon, for forcing me into this."

The fragrance of flowers—orange blossoms and freesias— filled the stone church in the seaside village as Amy entered through the open wooden doors on her father's arm. Against the stone walls the light from hundreds of slim white candles danced. And despite the smallness of the church, the pews were packed with people.

The intimate gathering wasn't the wedding she'd imagined— or planned. Yet the atmosphere was friendly. Joyous even— despite the fact that the Saxons were still in mourning.

Heads turned and faces lit up as Amy drifted past, doing her best to smile widely. But the heavy knot inside her stomach grew tighter with every step that she took. What would they all say if they knew the man good little virginal Amy had planned to marry had not fathered the baby in her womb? That the Saxon waiting for her at the end of the aisle was her baby's true father? Cold shivers rippled across her skin and shame curled inside her. It didn't bear thinking about.

And, most disturbing of all, was the man waiting at the altar.

The man she'd sworn that she despised last night.

Another lie. The powerful emotions Heath stirred in her might not be love, but nor were they hatred. They were linked to more basic feelings, instincts that it shamed her to possess.

It was herself she despised.

He stood at the end of the aisle alone, legs hip-width apart, his back to her. Tall, straight, clad in a dark suit that fit those shoulders without a wrinkle, he seemed remote, powerful. The filmy lace bridal veil had been folded back from her face, over her dark hair, and Amy could see him clearly. This wasn't the teen she'd known as a child…or the wild youth of her high school years. Nor was he the winemaker everyone called Black Saxon.

This was someone else altogether.

A powerful man. A saviour who had comforted her and held her in his arms through the worst night of her life. A lover who had made her forget her agony and taken her to heights of ecstasy she'd never known.

Memories of him had haunted her for the past two months. Making love with him would be no hardship. Just thinking about his touch caused her to turn to liquid…

Her lover drew her close, comforting her at first. Then, in a flash, it all changed. His mouth was cool against her hot flesh. Her head went back and a wild, keening sound escaped from her throat. He'd ripped away the ladylike veil to reveal someone she didn't know.

She reached the altar, the ivory silk taffeta whispering against her stockinged legs. Heath turned his head. The eyes that met hers were dark, serious, intent. He wasn't taking this marriage lightly. Her father placed her icy hand in Heath's, then he was gone, sliding into the first pew on the bride's side of the church, abandoning her into Heath's care.

The touch of Heath's fingers was hot against her cold hand. A slow warmth filled her. That uncanny connection. Amy swallowed.

Her lover shifted, a stab of pain followed. She flinched and tensed. He stilled and the tight tearing abated. "Don't stop," she whispered in a tone she didn't recognize as her own.

He moved again and pleasure buffeted her along, pain forgotten, as he wrapped her in strong arms. He moved against her…within her…with slow deliberate thrusts that caused the wildness to unravel within her. And she rushed headlong into the white heat that waited. It terrified her, this untrammelled passion. He'd turned her into someone she didn't know.

Heath had chosen to marry her and make her his bride. For the sake of a baby that he didn't know was his. She'd misled him. Deliberately. Her impulsive words came back to haunt her. She'd been in such turmoil….

"I'm pregnant, Heath."

She would never forget the expression on his face when she'd told him.

"You're sure?"

And then she'd given the answer she bitterly regretted. *"Three months pregnant."*

She had to tell him the truth. He would understand why she had misled him by adding an extra month, Amy thought. Heath knew her, Goody-Two-Shoes. He would realise how impossible it had been for her to confess to anyone that Roland was not the father of her the baby in her womb. And she hadn't wanted him to work out that he was the father of her child. Heath would never have suspected that she'd deliberately deceived him. She would tell him the truth—make it right.

She clung to his hand, drawing a startled glance. He gave her a quick wink and his serious expression dissolved.

The priest started to speak. Amy tensed. This was it. A squeeze from Heath's hand caused the clammy, disoriented sensation to recede and she started to feel a whole lot more upbeat. No one leaped out of the woodwork to demand that the ceremony be stopped, and the priest's familiar words washed over her. A choir of sweet voices sang one of her favourite arias, and a dreamy feeling of well-being seeped into Amy.

For the first time she started to believe that everything might work out.

When the time for the vows came, Heath passed her a card. She glanced at it and stiffened. Heath had written out new

vows. There was no mention of love. Only sharing, caring…
cherishing.

She glanced up at him, her eyes dewy with gratitude. Her
gaze lingered on the cheekbones that sloped sharply away
from those wicked eyes and the black-as-night hair. The hard,
rocklike features softened for an instant.

She'd told him how she felt about lying before God.
Had he changed their vows for her? Of course, it gave him
an out, too.

Now he didn't have to lie, either.

Afterwards, in the sunlit gardens of Saxon's Folly, in front
of the old white Victorian house where he'd grown up, Heath
played his part as the proud-new-husband as guests showered
both him and Amy with congratulations and wished them
many years of happiness together.

His mouth slanted at the irony.

If Amy'd had her way last night, today's wedding would
never have taken place. With his arm slung possessively around
Amy's shoulders, he led her to where a jazz ensemble played
smoky music from a rotunda set back between the Nikau palms.

"Would you like to dance?" he asked.

Amy hesitated. Not giving her a chance to demur, he took
her hand and hustled her into the grassy space, which posies
of white roses staked into the ground and joined by white and
silver ribbon marked out as the dance floor.

As he swept her into a waltz, the guests crowded closer.
Amy tensed in his arms and clutched his hand in a deathly grip.

"Relax," he murmured, smiling down at her. "Today's
supposed to be your day. Enjoy yourself."

"How can I?"

The late afternoon sunlight filtered through the fronds
overhead, casting gold splashes over her face. "Ignore everyone. Pretend it's just us."

"That scares me even more." But she smiled as she said it, and her grip on his fingers eased a tiny bit.

Other dancers joined them. Keeping his attention focused on her, he expertly threaded a path through them. "Listen to the band. Aren't they great?"

She nodded. "I thought so, too. They're one of the bands booked to play at the summer festival." After a beat she said, "There's so much to still do."

"I forbid you to think of work for the next five days." He softened the order with a smile, but he had every intention of making sure that Amy took it easy. It was about time someone pampered her a little; she'd been through so much.

She gave a soft sigh. "Easier said than done, but I'll do my best."

"Don't even consider packing a to do list. Or a pen."

That made her laugh. "I promise. And I won't even bring a laptop."

"I should hope not," he said darkly.

Amy giggled. She was moving fluidly now, graceful in the feminine wedding dress. Heath was astounded to discover that the bridal look turned him on. He wished he hadn't promised to wait. He would've loved to have peeled the ivory dress off her and revealed her naked skin and stockinged legs.

The fantasy made him grow all hot. By contrast, Amy seemed to have forgotten about her earlier tension. A burst of possessiveness rushed through him. She was his now. He would take care of her—and her baby.

She didn't even object as he drew her closer—ostensibly to avoid a pair of enthusiastic dancers. He didn't ease his hold, keeping her against him, enjoying the whiff of tuberose, her feminine softness as his thighs brushed hers under the gauzy wedding gown.

Bending his head, he asked, "Have I told you how beautiful you look today?"

Her head came up, her eyes startled. "No."

"You do."

Emotion flashed through her eyes. "Thank you."

Before he could say anything more, Ralph tapped him on the shoulder. He surrendered Amy to her father and watched as she danced away. This courting stuff was going to be hard on him, he suspected.

One step at time. Baby steps.

The rest of the day's festivities passed in a rush. The cutting of the cake. The tossing of the bouquet—which his sister caught—and the throwing of the garter to a pack of prowling males. Heath cast them a glare that warned them to keep their distance. They backed away, the tallest jumping up to snatch the prize when he flung it. Heath glared as the winner roared his triumph.

"Time to leave," he murmured to Amy.

The violet shadows under her eyes revealed the toll the day had taken on her. "Where are we going?"

It was the first time she'd shown any interest in their destination. He gave her a reckless grin. "You'll find out soon enough."

By the time she'd changed out of her wedding dress into a white pantsuit over a silk top and retrieved the bag she'd packed earlier, the helicopter was ready for them. For a moment Amy baulked on seeing it. "We're going in that?"

He nodded. "Of course."

"But—"

"Come," he knew he sounded impatient. But he was done going slow. He wasn't giving her any cause to refuse to go with him. "We need to leave now. I don't want to fly in the waning light."

"You're flying?"

He flashed his most devilish grin. "Yep."

"Oh."

But after that little breathy exclamation, there was no objection. She clambered in without another word. And her silent display of trust made Heath feel ten feet tall.

"Sit beside me."

She put on the headphones he gave her without argument. At first Amy was silent as he went through the preflight checks.

"Flick the switch."

She gave him a puzzled stare that turned to understanding as he gesticulated to the headphones she wore. She turned the switch and he could see her relief as the thumping noise of the rotors dulled.

"All set?" He said into the mouthpiece, and she nodded.

Once the helicopter lifted and swung, she gave a gasp. Beyond the bubble windows, their guests were waving.

Out of the corner of his eye, Heath watched her raise a hand and wave back. As they gained height, he saw that her hands were placed tightly over her harness, over her stomach.

The significance of that gesture hit him and his gut turned to mush. "Relax. Everything's going to be all right. Nothing will harm you—or the baby. I'd never take that risk."

The flight passed quickly. As Heath prepared to land, Amy said, "I always said I'd never fly in one of these contraptions."

"I remember." He'd offered her a trip many years ago.

"I valued my life." But he thought he detected a note of wistfulness. Had Amy wanted to fly with him back then when he'd first gotten his licence? She'd certainly never shown any desire to fly that he'd noticed. "I thought this thing would be the death of you one day," she added.

Heath didn't laugh. "I'm very careful."

"Good!"

He laughed then, amused by how much she managed to convey in that one word. Prim disapproval. He suppressed the urge to lean sideways and plant a kiss on her provocatively pursed lips and concentrated on bringing the bird down safely.

After the rotors had slowed, Amy said excitedly, "Oh, this

is Mataora. I can see the welcome sign. It's part of the Meitaki Islands, if I remember my geography right."

"You do. But we're not staying in the main resort," Heath said. "I've booked a bungalow on the beach."

As they stepped out, they were surrounded by well-trained staff who promised to secure the chopper, took their suitcases and led Amy and Heath to the open SUV that waited.

The drive to the bungalow didn't take long, and once they'd been settled, the welcoming committee departed after Amy refused their offers of elaborate alcoholic cocktails.

Suddenly the air felt very charged. In an effort to refuse the tension that had sprung up between them, Heath said, "You take the main bedroom, I'll take the other."

"There are two?"

He tried not to be insulted by the relief in her eyes. It was hard. "I thought you'd be more comfortable."

"Thanks, Heath."

Her gratitude grated. He'd much rather receive thanks with a husky note of satisfaction after lovemaking, than under these circumstances.

He sighed. They had five whole days together. Heath was determined that by the end of that period Amy would be at ease with him—and with the attraction that simmered between them. The hardest challenge of his life faced him: to convince Amy to fall in love with him.

Nine

When Amy emerged from her room the next morning, there was no sign of Heath in the luxurious sitting area or in the state-of-the-art galley kitchen. Hesitantly, she pushed open the door to his bedroom. It was empty.

A strange sense of desolation swept over her. Then she forced herself to rally. They were hardly the traditional honeymooners. They weren't even in love. This was a practical marriage, underpinned by practical considerations. So why was she feeling abandoned?

Heath wasn't seated on the sheltered deck outside the bungalow that overlooked the sea. Had he gone for a walk... without her? Or had he ventured to the main resort in search of entertainment that his wife could not provide?

Amy's shoulders had just sunk dejectedly when the call of her name made her straighten.

"You're awake." Heath came toward her, wearing dripping board shorts that clung to his thighs. The droplets of moisture on his water-slicked chest gleamed in the morning sun. And his black hair lay seal-sleek against his head.

Oh, my.

Amy didn't know where to look. The pleasure in his eyes made her forget all about her dejection of seconds ago. Flustered, her skin suddenly tight and hot, she couldn't think of a single intelligent thing to say.

Heath had no such problem. He flashed her a smile, his teeth white and straight in his tanned face. "The water's crisp and clear. Put on a swimsuit. I'll wait for you."

"I don't think I brought a swimsuit." Amy felt utterly foolish. She was usually so prepared. "I won't swim, I'll just watch." Then she blushed at how that sounded, and heat spiked through her at the notion of watching Heath in the water. "Uh…I'll bring my book."

Heath shrugged. "Whatever makes you happy." But Amy noticed the glow that had been in his eyes when he'd first greeted her had dimmed a little. Perhaps she could've been a little more enthusiastic. It made her feel like an utter killjoy. Yet she had no intention of joining a practically naked Heath in an ocean frolic.

Not while he roused such flames within her.

Good girls simply didn't play with fire.

There were worse ways to pass the morning than lounging in a deck chair on the beach reading, Amy decided an hour later. The only problem was that the book she'd packed was a sexy romance she'd been reading—and somewhere along the line the dark, sexy hero became Heath. It was inexplicable. It was discomforting.

Snapping the book shut, Amy shoved it back in her tote and shifted restlessly in the deck chair. Heath kept drawing her gaze like a magnet. His broad, bare shoulders gleamed like polished bronze in the sunlight whenever he stood full height in the shallows. Occasionally he would turn to face her, hesitate, then wave. Each time she felt just a tiny bit guilty at being caught looking, like a kid with a hand in the cookie jar. Finally, in danger of becoming mesmerized, she forced herself to look away. Adjusting her shades, she closed her eyes and fell into a half-dozing, half-dreaming state.

She started when cold droplets splashed onto her arm.

Heath stood beside her. Too big. Too naked. And far too close.

Amy's heart started to hammer. "Are you finished?"

"Mmm…it's not much fun swimming alone. There's sure to be a beachwear shop in the resort—we'll go buy you a swimsuit after lunch."

"Maybe." Amy wasn't sure that she was that keen on swimming alone with Heath. "But I'm not sure that I'll swim while we're here."

"Why not? I remember you being a very good swimmer when we used to splash around at the waterhole at the vineyard." He paused concern in his eyes. "Or did your doctor suggest that you give up swimming?"

"No, nothing like that." On the contrary, Dr. Shortt had said that swimming was a good form of exercise during her pregnancy. Cornered, she said, "Okay, we can look for a swimsuit."

The first thing that Heath discovered in the aptly named Splashes, the resort's boutique, was that he and Amy had opposing ideas on the nature of the swimwear she required.

"I can't possibly wear a bikini," she said in a scandalised whisper. "I'm pregnant."

"It's barely noticeable." He eyed her full breasts appreciatively, the only place where clear changes had taken place. "Try this one."

"Not that one. It's barely decent. And if it gets wet…" her voice trailed away.

Imagining the skimpy white fabric wet, clinging to her full breasts, was enough to make Heath grow hard. "That could be interesting," he said huskily.

"Heath!"

"Our bungalow is at the end of the beach. Pretty private." He shot her a simmering look. "Only I would see."

"That's one person too many. I'm not wearing it. Finished." The prim tone was back. And her colour was high.

"Fraidy cat," he murmured so softly that only she could hear. He took wicked satisfaction from making her blush. It delighted him. And meant she had to be aware of him.

She didn't answer back.

"What about this?" This time he took an outfit with a Lycra top in shades of pale rose pink and grape-coloured swirls with black piping and a black bikini bottom off the rack. Heath knew she looked good in romantic pinks and purples… and, more importantly, she wore them often.

Relief flooded her face. "The magenta is a bit bright. But much better than that," she said with a dark glance at the bikini before snatching the bits from his hands and heading for the fitting room.

Heath bit down on the urge to laugh. He'd forgotten how much he used to enjoy teasing Amy once she'd turned sixteen. He'd delighted in her wide eyes and her frowns of disapproval. It appeared that nothing had changed.

Except when she opened the doors, his breath snagged in his throat.

Everything had changed. This was no sixteen-year-old girl standing in front of him with curves in all the right places and defiant eyes. This was a woman. A woman he wanted. Badly.

"Don't you like it?" Amy asked when the silence stretched too long.

Heath almost choked. Like it? Hell, he loved it. "It'll do," he said instead. But he couldn't resist jerking her chain one last time. "If you're sure you don't want the white bikini?"

He could've sworn he heard a snort. But that wasn't

possible. Not from Amy Wright. Amy Saxon, he amended hastily. Hell, how could he have gotten that wrong?

"You get changed, and I'll meet you up front." Without waiting for an answer he made his way to the front of the boutique. He collected a wide-brimmed straw hat, a straw beach bag with a beach mat and a tube of sunscreen on the way. If she hadn't brought a swimsuit, she'd need those, too.

A dress that shimmered like liquid sunshine caught his eye. Somewhere between bronze and gold, the shade reminded him of Amy's eyes. He added the silky garment to the growing pile.

By the time Amy emerged with the swimsuit in hand, he'd already paid and was waiting in the front of the store, a large silver bag in his hand.

She stopped dead. "I was going to pay for that myself."

He waved a dismissive hand. "It's done."

Her mouth pursed.

"A gift for my beautiful bride. Put your purse away and thank me instead," he said, while the shop assistant looked on with an indulgent smile.

"Thank you," Amy said far more sweetly than he expected. He'd expected gritted teeth at the very least.

He leaned toward her. "And my kiss?"

Heath knew he was being deliberately provocative. He was pushing her buttons. He wanted a response; he wanted to see her precious eyes shooting sparks at him. But he knew it was highly unlikely. Amy always behaved perfectly.

No reason to expect anything different this time.

Even if he was taunting her.

Her expression didn't change. The first indication he had that not all was as it had always been was the way she swayed toward him, her lashes lowered. Instead of the hesitant peck on the check that he'd expected, her lips puckered into a sultry moue and landed squarely on his mouth. Soft. Sweet. Heath's heart started to pound in his chest.

Her mouth was soft and her lips moved just enough under his to give him an idea of what he was missing out on by giving a promise to give her time.

A long moment later she stepped away, her eyes flicking to the shop attendant, revealing that she was as aware as he of their audience.

"Thank you, my darling," she murmured throatily.

Touché. Amy taking risks was a very dangerous woman. To Heath's utter disgust he found that he was sweating.

That evening the air was heavy with the distinctive fragrance of frangipani from the shrubs that grew in lush profusion around the bungalow. Amy sat in one of the cane armchairs grouped on the wooden deck and tried to appear relaxed as she leaned back against the plumped-up cushions, no easy feat with Heath towering in front of her, his back to the ocean as he leaned against the wooden balustrade.

Holding her gaze, Heath raised his glass.

"To my bride."

The words resounded in the velvety dusk. A melting sensation rushed through Amy. She hadn't forgotten the way his eyes had skimmed her swimsuit-clad body in Splashes boutique earlier. In fact, odd tingles shot through her every time she thought about it, even though she tried very hard to avoid thinking about it at all. Yet she couldn't seem to help herself. She couldn't forget how his eyes had been dark one moment then bright with carnal desire the next. The transformation had taken her breath away. It had been shocking…but exciting too. And it had awakened worrying wanting feelings in her.

She didn't *want* to want Heath.

"Thank you," she managed a husky response to his toast and took a quick sip of the mineral water she'd opted for in place of champagne from the elegant tulip-shaped glass, then wondered what to say next.

Despite the fact that the resort felt like a place for lovers, honeymooners, she didn't feel like a bride. But she couldn't confess that. It wasn't his fault. It was hers. Perhaps he expected a toast in return? She shot him a furtive little look from under her lashes.

"To—" She broke off awkwardly. *To my groom.* No, she couldn't bring herself to say it. He wasn't the groom of her heart. "To our marriage," she offered instead, a little lamely.

"To our marriage," he echoed, his voice deep.

The glow of candles spilled through the large picture windows from the bungalow and suffused his features with a golden cast, highlighting his bottom lip, throwing his eyes into deep relief. All gold light and dark shadows. A sexy, brooding stranger.

A frisson rippled through her.

Stop it, she told herself. This was Heath. No stranger. She'd known him all her life. There was no reason for her heart to be fluttering in her chest, no reason to be apprehensive about the *a deux* dinner he'd arranged. They weren't even alone, for heaven's sake. A chef was preparing their meal in the kitchen. A few minutes ago a waiter clad in white, except for a striped butcher's apron, had appeared armed with a bottle of champagne, the champagne that Heath was drinking, and that Amy had refused, conscious of the life within her.

But Heath was staring at her, unsettling her.

"Your hair suits you like that," he said.

She smoothed her hand over the tousled locks. "It's a mess." She'd taken a shower and changed into the gauzy bronze dress that Heath had bought for her. It had seemed the perfect choice for the balmy night. Then Heath had knocked on the door to advise her that the catering staff would be there in five minutes. She hadn't had a chance to blow-dry her hair into its usual bob. Instead she'd focused on a quick fix—a dab of hair mousse, moisturizer on her cheeks, a brush of mascara and a soft pink lip gloss.

"I like it."

A thrill of pleasure rushed through her at his compliment. Followed by something else, something infinitely more dangerous.

He moved closer. She stiffened and quickly drained her drink.

"Here, let me take that."

For a moment she held onto the empty glass, reluctant to surrender it. The glass gave her something to hold, sipping the water gave her something to do, creating a barrier between them. With the glass gone, he would be even closer.

Reluctantly, she released it. He set her glass down on a glass-topped table and turned back.

Amy was on her feet, a strange cat-on-a-hot-tin-roof edginess making her say hurriedly, "Let's walk to the water's edge."

He gave her a strange look. "There isn't enough time. Dinner will be ready shortly."

"Oh." He had her there. She tripped toward the railing and, resting her hands on the wood, stared across the pale beach at the sea glimmering in the waning light.

"Do you really want to walk now?" He was right behind her. "Perhaps after dinner?"

"It was just an idea," she said, her voice suddenly husky. Not a brilliant one. But then escape had been at the forefront of her mind, driven by the need to protect herself from the restless edginess his proximity evoked.

And what had it gained her? He was closer now. Even though he wasn't touching her, she felt crowded, trapped between his body and the balustrade. Her heart leaped. He was too close. There was no escape.

Yet it was strange to be thinking of Heath trying to besiege her. She was hardly his type. The bad boy never dated good girls. But he'd been her friend, kind of, once upon a time. And now he was the father of her child, she reminded herself.

Her husband, too.

Her hands gripped the wooden railing. The fact that he was her husband should have made it easier to cope with the disturbing feelings he aroused in her. It didn't. It only made it worse.

This kind of pervasive desire was supposed to come parcelled up with love. It devastated her to realise it wasn't. She certainly didn't love Heath.

But she wanted him. It was disturbing—shocking—to feel this way about him. It was as if her body had been taken over by a force she did not recognise. And she didn't like it one little bit.

It was wrong to feel this way about him.

She'd loved Roland—

"I don't want to go anywhere," he whispered against the exposed skin behind her ear, causing shivers to riot down her spine. "I want to stay right here."

Amy whirled around. "Heath—"

His arms came around her. Amy's breath left her in a whoosh of air. Then she realised that the focus of his attention lay beyond her, behind her. She stilled. When his hands returned to in front of her, he held a spray of frangipani between his long, blunt fingers—winemaker's hands—and the night was full of heady tropical scent.

"Stand still."

The command was not necessary. Amy couldn't have moved if she'd tried. Her knees felt weak. Her senses were overpowered by him, holding her captive. She hoped desperately that her ragged breathing wouldn't betray her. His fingers touched her ear. Amy started, and adrenalin exploded in a rush into her veins as he slid the frangipani blooms into her hair.

"There," Heath stepped back and suddenly Amy could breathe again. Until he smiled. Her heart twisted and for a moment she swayed toward him.

Heath was safe. As long as she could keep it straight in her head that desire had nothing to do with love, as long as her mind didn't start playing tricks on her, and have her imagining she was falling in love with Heath…everything would be fine.

She'd be safe.

Her silly, trampled-on heart would be safe, too.

And she and Heath didn't need love to bind them together. They had the baby. The baby he believed was his brother's.

Her stomach rolled over and a sick sensation assailed her. She needed to tell him about that…

But not now.

Not when his head was coming toward her with that mellow gleam in his hellfire, bad-boy eyes and an irresistible smile turning up the corners of his mouth. But the sound of a footfall gave him pause, and they both turned to find the waiter indicating that dinner was served.

Dinner was done, and the resort staff had departed.

Heath lounged back on the sofa in the living room and his smile widened as Amy's throat bobbed as she swallowed.

She was nervous. Good. He wanted to keep her off balance. He didn't want her starting to harbour brotherly thoughts of him.

"Come to me," he whispered softly. For a brief instant he thought she was going to say something, refuse even, then with a sigh she came.

She stood before him, her eyes lowered, and even in the subdued glow of the candlelight he could see that she was trembling.

Heath frowned.

"What are you afraid of?"

Her eyelids shot open and her wild, golden gaze met his. The impact made him shudder. Heath's breathing quickened as he scooped her onto his lap, her thighs straddling his hips. Her scent enveloped him, she smelled of roses and raw passion.

It wasn't fear that was causing her to tremble. It was desire.

He was already hard, his erection straining against the front of his trousers.

Before she could object to the intimacy of the close contact, he threaded his hands through her silken, tousled hair and pulled her close. Her lips met his, lush and soft, and he groaned aloud.

Their mouths met, kissed, parted and returned to kiss again. An erotic dance. One that left Heath aching for more.

Cupping her head between his work-worn hands, he eased her closer to taste the sweetness of her mouth…again and again.

"I will never tire of this," he whispered against her lips.

Amy made a soft, satisfied sound, almost a purr of delight.

In response, Heath freed her hair and stroked his hands over her bare shoulders, which shimmered in the candle glow and down her back, over the sleek fabric of the bronze dress.

Then, one-handed, he yanked his shirt from his trousers and impatiently undid the buttons so that the shirt fell open, baring his chest.

Amy's gasp of awe, followed by the stroke of a lone fingertip along the centre of his breastbone caused his erection to leap in response.

"Touch me," he demanded, wrapping his arms around her, drawing her a little closer and letting his fingers play along the indent of her spine.

Both her hands came down on the bare skin of his torso and traced the straining pectoral muscles before sliding down to explore the ridges of his abdomen.

He closed his eyes and hissed through clenched teeth, a sound of suppressed delight.

When he opened his eyes, he stared straight into golden ones glinting with curiosity and hunger.

"I didn't see you last time." A hectic flush coloured her cheeks.

Last time they'd been surrounded by night. Heath's hands stilled. Last time…

He'd brought her to Chosen Valley, shocked and shaken after surviving the car accident that had injured his brother. Barely bruised, she'd shivered with reaction. Finally, he'd given her a mild sedative and crawled in beside her, holding her until she warmed and her teeth stopped clattering, until she eased into a restless sleep.

Long before dawn he'd left her sleeping under Josie's supervision and gone to the hospital to see how Roland was faring in intensive care. His brother had passed away while he was there.

Distraught, he'd driven home, dismissed Josie and broken the news of Roland's death to Amy.

Her grief had been palpable. He'd held her in the predawn darkness…and then the raging grief had exploded into something else. Instead of comforting her, he'd loved her under the cover of darkness.

It had been the only way to stanch their grief.

He would never regret making love to her.

"Look all you want," he murmured now.

The smile she bestowed on him was confident…sensual… intensely womanly. "You bet I will."

Heath's fingers slid beneath the shoestring ties of the bronze dress and worked them loose. The dress fell away, pooling around her hips. Leaning forward he kissed the smooth, white-marble skin, the dark tips of her full-blown breasts, revelling in the throaty moans she made.

She was so sensitive, so responsive. His arousal skyrocketed, and he knew that if he didn't act soon it would all be over before it had even started.

Loosening his zipper he slid his pants down over his hips. Then he drew Amy close. He felt her start as his rocklike hardness nestled against her secret places.

He stroked her bare back with his palms. She was quivering with expectation. And Heath's tight control gave.

"Look at me," he said hoarsely.

Her eyes clashed with his, glazed with passion. Staring into the molten-gold depths, Heath slid his hands under the hem of her dress.

When he discovered the minuscule thong she was wearing, his heart nearly gave out. She gave him that tantalizing, slow smile again and his pulse thundered. He ran two fingers under the barely decent strings and found her slick wetness.

His breath caught in his throat and his body surged forward. The thong snapped. Her eyes went wide.

Heath held her hips, lifting her, positioning her. The catch of her breath made him shudder. And an instant later her hot heat closed around him.

Heath groaned. And then she was sliding against him, the motions causing silver bursts of sensation to explode through him even as the rippling shivers took her over the edge.

Ten

Heath woke through slow degrees.

His first thought was for Amy. He turned his head. She was still sleeping. In the faded pink of the morning light, her dark eyelashes fanned down against her pale skin and one of her hands rested between the pillow and her cheek.

After they'd made love last night, she'd been silent and had avoided Heath's gaze.

He'd tried to draw her out, to no avail. She'd delayed going to bed and had finally fallen asleep on the sofa. He'd carried her to bed.

Had Amy regretted being swept away by the passion that simmered so hotly between them? Had she felt as though she'd betrayed Roland…for a second time?

He'd promised Amy time.

And had broken that promise. Two nights after making their vows he'd taken her. Taken her…

Just thinking of what his hunger—what he'd done—caused

him to tense in shame. Yes, she'd responded to his loving. Carnally. Voraciously even. That was not the point.

"As for knowing me…you don't know this me. I don't even know this side of me—it's embarrassing."

The point was she didn't want to feel this hunger for him. Her words came back to haunt him. She'd feel ashamed. And he'd done that to her. All because he was too damned impatient to wait. Because he wanted her. To brand her as his. And in doing so he might've risked losing her.

He'd given no quarter last night. He'd taken her, intending to imprint himself on her, so that she would never forget.

Pure male possessiveness.

Mine.

How could he expect her to ever trust his word again?

Later, after an English breakfast complete with fried eggs, bacon, toast and marmalade, they drove to a beach that was supposed to be magnificent. With the straw beach bag Heath had bought for her slung over her shoulder, Amy followed him down a narrow pathway. The moment they came through the trees Heath stopped dead.

Amy bumped into his legs and instantly felt a flutter of heat at the unexpected physical contact.

"Sorry," she muttered.

"Don't apologise." Heath turned his head, the tanned skin drawn tight across his cheekbones. She couldn't read the expression in his eyes behind the dark lenses of his Wayfarers.

This stilted discomfort had been there since they'd woken up. There had been a distance between them. And Amy had known she'd missed the chance to tell him that the baby was his. It would be much harder now that they'd made love.

Breathlessly she asked, "Is this the right beach?"

He stared at her unblinkingly until she started to feel uncomfortable.

"Oh, yes, this is the right beach."

So what was the problem? Amy glanced past him to the deserted strip of golden sand and dark turquoise sea. "Then why are we stopping?"

"I'm not sure this is a good idea."

"Why?" Amy frowned. The beach looked like a still from an advertisement for paradise. "Is it unsafe?"

"You could say that."

Amy narrowed her eyes against the morning sun glittering off the water looking for flat sections of water, that might signal a riptide or something equally ominous. "I can't see anything wrong, it looks idyllic to me." She turned worried eyes on Heath. "What's the problem?"

He took his time answering. "Not enough people." He looked at her from under hooded eyelids.

And then it hit her. He didn't want to be alone with her. The first thing she felt was hurt. She shrugged it off. Did he regret making love last night?

Pretending that she hadn't gotten his point, she strode forward. "Well, we don't need to swim. The concierge was right, it's beautiful," she flung over her shoulder. "We can just soak up the sun and the peace away from the crowds."

Halting at the edge of the sea, Amy pulled a straw mat out of her bag, unrolled it, and laid it down. She was aware of Heath behind her, but she pretended not to notice his presence.

Slipping off the loose-fitting, crinkled-cotton pink dress with shoestring ties to reveal the bathing suit Heath had bought for her, she slathered on sunscreen, then she stretched herself out on the mat.

There was dead silence from behind her.

At first it rattled her nerves, and she fought the urge to peer through her lashes and see what Heath was doing. But as the silent seconds stretched into minutes, she began to relax.

If Heath thought there was safety in numbers, she'd prove

to him he was perfectly safe on this deserted beach with her. She certainly wasn't going to fall all over him.

It wasn't her style.

So Amy lay with her eyes closed, her hands behind her head, absorbing the sun's heat. She must have dozed a little, because a while later she stirred at the sound of Heath's voice asking whether she needed more sunscreen.

"Mmm," she murmured, more asleep than awake.

The shock of his hands on her legs woke her with a start. "What are you doing?"

He gave her a barbed smile. "Putting sunscreen on you. You asked, didn't you?"

"I thought you meant to pass me the bottle."

"My hands were already oily. No sense in two of us getting sticky," he said with horrible logic.

"I suppose so," she said, reluctant pleasure creeping through her as he applied the lotion in long, lazy strokes. "That's far enough," Amy objected when his slippery fingers skirted the high-cut legs of the bikini bottoms.

"If you say so." His eyes glittered. "These bits of skin often get overlooked and burn badly." His fingers swept under the edge of the stretchy fabric and she leaped to a sitting position as if she'd been electrified.

"Give me that cream."

He surrendered it, and Amy knew his black-devil's eyes would be laughing behind the Wayfarers, damn him!

He lay back, his elbows propped in the sand behind him, tanned skin gleaming in the sun, and watched her through half-closed eyes.

Self-consciousness rippled through Amy. Her fingers hesitated for a moment then she forced herself to rub cream into her arms and shoulders with brisk circular movements.

"Careful you don't rub your skin off. You sure you don't

want me to do it for you? I'll be much more gentle." There was amusement in his voice.

She ignored him and squirted more cream into her hand with unnecessary vigour. Peeling the bottom hem of the tank top up, she slathered on cream across the strip of skin above her black bikini briefs. The cream was cold against her sun-warmed stomach. Amy caught her breath. She heard Heath gasp, too.

When she looked up, Heath sat upright, his eyes blazing. "Did the baby move?" he asked hoarsely.

"No, the cream was cold." She rubbed the last remnants in as she offered the humdrum explanation.

"Oh, I thought—" For a moment he looked uncertain, then he dropped back into the lounging lazy position in the sand. "I thought it was the baby. Have you felt it move yet?"

She shook her head. "I saw it move on the scan at my last appointment. But I haven't felt it yet. It's kind of strange. Dr. Shortt says I will in a couple of weeks."

"Tell me when it happens."

Amy let the high-handedness go. He cared. He really cared. And that warmed her more than she'd ever expected. He was complicated, her husband. He never did quite what she expected.

"You missed one spot."

"What?" She stared at him blankly.

"You need some sunscreen on your—" he broke off "—on your chest." His voice had gone all raspy.

She glanced down at the pale bare skin that the neckline of the magenta-and-pink tank top framed.

"I suppose." She wasn't wildly keen to touch the sloping flesh of her breasts—not with Heath watching. Not with last night's wild lovemaking still so fresh in her mind.

"Do you want me to do it for you?"

Amy glared at him. Those darn sunshades. She couldn't read his expression. But from the way her breasts tingled, she suspected that was where his gaze was fixed.

"Heath, stop it! You're making me feel self-conscious."

"Sorry." Instantly he was contrite. "I promised you time—and I broke my word."

Broken his word? He was talking about last night, Amy realised. He felt guilty. That he'd pushed her too soon. Didn't he know it took two to tango? That she'd been as guilty—if that was the right word—as he was?

Before she could say anything, he'd pushed himself to his feet, his taut stomach muscles rippling in the sun.

"I need to cool off."

Amy suspected that he meant that in more ways than one. Perhaps this was exactly what he'd feared when he'd realised the beach was deserted. Perhaps she'd been mistaken when she'd thought he hadn't wanted to be alone with her. The ache of hurt she'd experienced vanished.

Amy watched as Heath loped into the shallows and sank into the lapping wavelets. Driven by a fresh sense of energy, she jumped to her feet and ran into the water.

As his head surfaced, she swept her hand through the salty water sending up a spray that hit him squarely in the face. He sputtered.

Amy laughed.

"I'll get you for that!"

Just before she started to swim, she called out, "Catch me if you can."

That set the tone for the rest of the day. They laughed and joked and Amy found herself looking forward to the night to come. There was no doubt in her mind that they would be making love again tonight.

There was an electric awareness between them, a sense of waiting. Heath would look at her with heat in his eyes when he thought she hadn't seen, and glance away when her gaze caught his.

It cut two ways. Because every time she scanned his long lean body and remembered the sleekness of his naked skin against hers last night, heat would sear her and her breathing would quicken. The strength of the physical thread between them held them both equally ensnared.

Amy had never imagined anything like it.

But nor had she imagined enjoying time alone with Heath this much. They laughed. They talked. He listened to what she had to say and treated her opinions with a respect that she'd never received from Roland. The silent admission felt like treachery, but it was true. Heath exhibited a caring, a respect, toward her that was enormously seductive.

That night, he arranged to take her out for an early dinner to a popular restaurant on the island.

Amy was wearing the bronze dress again. It was so comfortable, but so liberating too. She'd never owned anything as sophisticated. Other than her gold locket and the ring Heath had given her, she wore no jewellery. But the dress didn't need more. Heath's eyes told her that as his gaze stroked over her.

"You're beautiful, Amy."

She felt the colour surge in her cheeks. "It's the dress you bought," she bubbled. "I'd never thought of wearing this colour before."

"Oh, no." He was shaking his head. "It's you, Amy-love. You're beautiful."

The blush intensified. Not for the first time, she wished she could control it. That her skin wasn't such an obvious barometer of her every emotion. No one had ever called her beautiful before. Pretty, yes. Feminine. Well-groomed and stylish. But never beautiful.

But there was no doubt that Heath was sincere—it radiated from him. He truly believed she was beautiful.

And she wasn't disabusing him of that belief.

"The car is here," she said with relief as an engine purred beyond the bungalow windows, breaking the quiet of the island evening.

The evening passed too quickly. Amy glowed under Heath's attention, hardly noticing the staggering array of seafood on the buffet, picking at morsels of oyster and squid, barely tasting a thing.

A dreamy state encapsulated her. She felt as if she'd stepped into someone else's body for the night. Until she met Heath's gaze and felt the desire bolt through her.

Reality crashed in. There was no doubt that this was her body. She was becoming accustomed to the hunger that he aroused in her sometimes with only a look. The shame was finally starting to recede.

She was married to the man. He was her husband. She was pregnant with his baby.

All day she'd been putting off telling him, not wanting to spoil the unspoken truce that hovered, so fragile, between them. *Just give me tonight.*

That's all she wanted. One more night. A little more time to cement the accord that was slowly building between them. Until that awful night of Roland's death, she'd never done anything wrong in her life.

Since then, it seemed she'd done nothing right.

Sleeping with a man she wasn't married to the night the man she loved had died. Agreeing to marry a man she didn't love. And omitting to tell him that the baby she carried in her womb was his. The catalogue of sins was serious. So serious that she'd borne them all alone.

"Just one more day, please," she prayed hoping that a higher power would give her the time. "I'll never do anything wrong in my life again."

The bargaining appeared to work. The accumulated years of good deeds must've held up. Because Heath kept watching her with smiling, approving eyes and listening to her with his full attention. Heady stuff. Amy could've sworn that the fruit juice she'd drunk had gone to her head. She felt light-headed, a touch dizzy with delight.

It was when she rose to her feet that the pain hit her.

"Heath!" She grabbed his sleeve as she doubled over.

"Are you okay?"

"I'm not sure," she gasped. The spasm passed. She straightened cautiously. Another piercing pain surged through her. And panic followed. "No, I'm not okay."

"Where's the pain?" he asked urgently.

"My stomach."

He blanched, his lips paling. "The baby?"

Heath voiced the words she hadn't even dared think.

"I don't know!" A worse wave of dizziness shook her as another spasm hit her. "Heath, I want to go home."

"I'll get you home."

Turning his head, he summoned a waiter. Within a minute he had her in the car.

Misery consumed Amy.

The baby...

She hadn't wanted it. She'd resented its presence—tangible evidence of the mistake she'd made. And now her belly was full of pain. She didn't deserve to keep her baby. A sob broke from her throat.

Heath's arm steadied her. "There's no doctor on the island at the moment, Amy. But there's a nurse. She's meeting us at the airfield."

"The airfield?"

"As long as she says it's safe, I'm taking you home. I'll do everything in my power to see that you don't lose your baby."

* * *

Dr. Shortt folded up his stethoscope and straightened from examining Amy on the large bed in Heath's navy–and–dull gold bedroom back at Chosen Valley.

"The island nurse was correct. It *is* food poisoning. Amy will need rest and plenty of fluids over the next few days."

"And the baby?" Anxiety balled in Heath's chest. The baby was her last connection to his brother. Even though she hadn't wanted to be pregnant, Heath had no doubt that losing the baby now would devastate Amy.

Dr. Shortt gave a sigh. "It depends on what bacteria caused it. There are some nasties out there that can affect the fetus. I'll take samples and the lab will do a culture. It will be a couple of days before we have a result."

"A couple of days?" said Amy faintly from the bed. "Do we have to wait so long?"

"Yes," said the doctor.

"It must have been the buffet dinner," said Amy.

"Unlikely," replied Dr. Shortt. "The bacteria had probably already been in your system for at least eight hours before you started to feel ill. More likely breakfast."

"I had eggs over easy and bacon," said Amy.

"That's a possibility." Dr. Shortt nodded. "Now don't forget to drink plenty of fluids—and call me if the cramps return or grow more severe."

"Could I still miscarry?"

The doctor hesitated before saying very gently, "If it's a bug like listeria, that's possible. Miscarriage usually occurs within twenty-four hours."

"Oh," Amy fell silent.

Heath spared her a glance. Her face was pasty, her skin dewy with perspiration. She'd been running a fever earlier. That, along with a headache, nausea and vomiting had made the trip in the helicopter back from Mataora a nightmare journey for her.

He hurried to her side, tenderness overwhelming him. "You just take it easy, Amy-love."

She gave him a wan smile. "Thank you for taking my worst fears so seriously."

"Always," he vowed, holding her gaze for a long moment. Then he turned his attention to the portly figure of the doctor. "Thank you for coming out."

"I'm sorry it was under such circumstances. Call me if you have any concerns. Otherwise I'll pop by in the morning to check on Amy." He made his way out.

When the doctor had closed the door behind him, Heath closed his fingers around Amy's. He wanted to tell her how worried he'd been about her, how the nightmare flight back had seemed to take forever. Instead, forcing a cheerful note, he said, "A few days and you'll be as right as rain."

"And my baby?" Her gold eyes held terror.

"We'll take that one day at a time. For now let's concentrate on getting you well and back on your feet."

Heath didn't voice his own fear: that if she lost this baby, then the whole reason for their marriage vanished, too. Heath clenched his fists.

There would be no reason for Amy to stay married to him. None at all.

He would do everything in his power to make sure that her baby survived. Without the baby, he'd lose her for sure.

Eleven

Three days later Amy felt weak and washed out, but the debilitating nausea and vomiting had finally passed.

She began to fret about wrecking the honeymoon that Heath had seemed to want so much, about missing work, about the approaching summer festival. But it didn't matter how much she fretted or what she said, Heath would not allow her to rise from the big bed in the master suite at Chosen Valley.

For once his take-charge behaviour didn't grate. Amy was silently relieved to be told to take time off for her weak-as-water body to recover.

There wasn't even the opportunity to get bored. Over the past three days she'd had plenty of visitors. Her father. Heath's parents. Alyssa and Joshua. And Megan. Everyone was so concerned about her, despite her constant reassurances that she would be fine. Although, to be truthful, her stomach still ached and she was sure that she must have lost at least ten pounds.

The tests came back confirming that she'd been infected

by salmonella bacteria and Dr. Shortt popped in on the fourth morning to check her over. After he'd checked the tympanic thermometer and declared her temperature normal, he carefully explained that there would be no risk to her baby.

Joy and relief flooded Amy.

"You're sure?" she asked, desperate for reassurance.

He nodded.

Amy felt as if a gigantic weight had been taken off her shoulders, as if she'd been granted a reprieve from a sentence too awful to think about.

After the doctor had left, Amy fell back against the plumped pillows and stared out the window across to the green hills in the distance and counted her blessings.

At what point had the baby become so important to her? Her teeth gnawed her bottom lip. When had she stopped wishing that she wasn't pregnant and started to accept the life growing within her body? She laid a hand on the burgeoning bump of her stomach. Somewhere along the way, she'd started looking forward to the birth. Had it been on the day that Heath had given her that exquisite engagement ring and taken her to the aquarium? Maybe.

Her musings were interrupted when the bedroom door banged open and Megan burst in.

"How are you feeling today, sister?"

Amy beamed at Heath's energetic sister. "Wonderful. Dr. Shortt assures me that there will be no lasting damage from this bout of food poisoning. I'm so relieved."

"Oh, great!" Megan came and gave her a hug. "I'm thrilled for you and Heath. When's the baby due?"

"End of June." Amy touched her tummy. She couldn't seem to stop. "I've even got a baby bump to prove it."

Delight spread over Megan's face. "We'll have to go shopping. I've never shopped for maternity clothes before. Or cribs. Or strollers." Megan rubbed her hands in glee.

Amy started to laugh helplessly. "I hadn't even thought about all that." Heath wouldn't want to come. By telling him she was three months' pregnant instead of two, she'd effectively caused him to believe that the baby was Roland's. There'd be no reason for him to want to come. "I'd love to have your help. I'm glad you're here, Megan. All my life I wanted a sister."

"Me, too. Although I love my brothers, believe it or not."

"What's not to love about your brothers?" Whenever she'd spent time at Saxon's Folly, Amy had gone home wishing she'd had siblings.

"Now you're part of the family," Megan said generously. "We're all glad for you and Heath. He's so happy."

That startled Amy. She hadn't noticed a difference. "Heath's happy?"

"Walking on air. He's so in love with you it's sweet."

Megan believed Heath loved her?

Amy gave Megan an uncertain smile. "Glad you think it's sweet."

Megan placed her forefinger over her lips. "Don't let my brother hear I described him as sweet. He's gotten far too used to his Bad Saxon image." Megan wandered over to the dresser and pinched a dab of Heath's Eau Savage cologne. "We couldn't believe it when he broke the news that you were getting married."

Amy waited tensely.

"Mother was worried. Heath assured her he'd only asked you to marry him because he loved you."

Heath loved her.

The rest of Megan's visit passed in a blur of chatter that Amy didn't even absorb. Megan finally rushed off and Amy stared at the white plastered ceiling, her brain working overtime.

After the first shock wore off, Amy discovered that Megan's revelation had caused a huge shift in her thinking. It cast a whole new complexion on Heath's behaviour. She thought about the attention he showered her with on Mataora, his concern during her illness. She remembered the way he smiled at her, the tenderness that sometimes glowed in his eyes.

That was love.

A lightness came over her. Suddenly the future seemed brighter. She liked the idea of Heath loving her.

When the door opened again a little later, Heath stood there, tall and dark and so gorgeously male that her hormones went into overdrive. Amy's heart twisted over and she sent him a smile full of tender joy.

"You're looking better," he said, his eyes lightening as he scanned her features, his inspection warming her. "Would you like me to carry you downstairs? The sitting room is pleasant and sunny. I can open the doors to let some of the summer in. A little later, when it gets dark, we can put on the Christmas tree lights."

"That sounds lovely. But honestly, I can walk."

His black eyes sparkled. "You don't need to."

Advancing on her, he swept her up in his arms and Amy gave herself up to his strength. Nestled close to his heart, surrounded by the lemon-and-oakmossy masculine scent of him, she clung to his broad shoulders as he headed down the stairs. Once in the living room, he lowered her onto the plush velvet sofa. Shafts of December sunlight fell in broad golden bands across the Kelim rug, giving the room a glorious warmth.

"I'll get you a mohair throw for your legs."

"I'm fine," she protested, "honestly."

But he disappeared into the hall and she heard him rummaging in the hall cupboard.

Amy was starting to realise that Heath looked after his own and would never let her down. Her father had been right when he'd said that Heath was always where he was needed, solid as an ancient oak. She'd been blind to that side of him.

What else had she missed?

Heath had once joked that she could have picked him to be the man she loved. She'd dismissed it. Now she couldn't help considering whether, in the blinkered way of youth, she'd chosen the wrong guy.

Roland had been older. Glamorous. She'd been blinded by his sophistication. In love with the notion of being in love. And she'd been wary of Heath's bad boy image—and he'd already been gaining a reputation as a love-'em-and-leave-'em type. Not quite what she'd wanted with her naive dreams of a princely groom and white wedding night.

So maybe Heath hadn't given her the virginal wedding night her young heart had fantasised about. But he'd made her first time something special—even though it had been at a time when her world was falling apart. He'd given her something to cling to in the days—weeks—that followed Roland's death.

They'd conceived a child.

When he came back, he covered her legs and sank down on the sofa set at right angles to the one where she sat.

"Dr. Shortt called to tell me that he'd visited you this morning and gave you a clean bill of health."

Amy nodded. "Yes, he says it was salmonella."

"He told me—and he said that the baby would be fine."

Amy gave Heath a beatific smile. "It's such a relief. I'd started to feel like every way I turned things were going awry. Everything seems to be coming right again." Like the discovery that he loved her. She paused, wondering how best to broach that. Finally, she said, "Your sister came to visit this morning, too."

Heath raised his eyebrows. "I suppose she showered you with gossip about the summer festival and got you all fired up about getting back to work?"

"Well, it *is* only a five days away now."

"Don't worry about it, *Amy-love,* it's all under control. Alyssa and Mom and I have all been tying up the final loose ends."

Amy hesitated. But the endearment Amy-love spurred her on. "Megan told me something very interesting."

"What was that?" Heath didn't sound particularly interested in what his sister had to say.

A silence. Then Amy said softly, "She told me that you're in love with me."

For a moment Heath's expression didn't change, then all the emotion drained out, leaving it devoid of all expression.

After a moment he said, "And you believed her?"

Her heart thudded in her throat. Megan was often tactless, but she was also brutally honest. "She was very convincing."

He didn't look like a man in love. The sinking sensation in her stomach confirmed that Megan must've had it all wrong.

Amy swallowed desperately. Had she made a terrible mistake confronting him with his sister's opinions? No, she hadn't. They were married. She deserved the truth. "Are you denying it?" she asked bravely.

"I'm certainly not admitting it." There was an angry edge to his tone. "Amy, you shouldn't believe everything my family says. Of course, they think I love you. I've made damn sure they believe that. What other reason could I give them for marrying you?"

All the joy and confidence escaped Amy like helium from a child's balloon. "Didn't they believe you were doing it for the sake of Roland's child?"

He shot her a bitter look. "That's what you believed. They would've hated that."

"What do you mean?"

"Oh, Amy, that would've worried my mother to death. She would've been so concerned for both of us. I can see her trying to talk us out of the marriage. At least this way, by thinking I loved you and that I was going to help you through the grief of Roland's death, it gave my family hope that this mad marriage would work."

Mad marriage? Her heart sank. "But it can work." Amy felt as though she were wading through quicksand. Every way she moved, the situation became worse. "It has to work."

"For the baby's sake. I know." His voice was flat, his eyes empty of all emotion. "Don't worry, Amy, I'm not going to desert you."

"I know that. I trust you, Heath."

Emotion leaped in his eyes like flame. Then it went out like a doused candle. "Do you? Really?"

"Yes." She sucked in air. "I was wrong about you in the past when I thought you were wild and reckless and unreliable. I didn't see the real you."

"But you do now?" There was a twist to his mouth that she didn't much like. "Because my sister told you I was in love with you?"

"Okay, I shouldn't have believed it. It's rubbish, I accept that."

"It's not love that ties us together, Amy-love. It's something a lot more basic."

She flinched at the mocking use of what she'd considered an endearment until a few minutes ago.

When he came toward her with swift, panther strides, every muscle in her body tensed. The kiss he bestowed on her surprised mouth was ruthless and by the time he'd finished Amy was breathing hard.

"That's what binds us together. It's not called love. You'll never love me and—"

"Don't say it." Amy covered her ears. She didn't want to hear him denigrating the tenderness that had grown between them during their honeymoon, didn't want to hear it labelled by some crude word.

It hurt to hear the edge in him. Clearly he didn't love her— had never loved her. Desperate to bridge the chasm between them, Amy said, "Don't let's fight. And don't let's forget that there's the baby, too. A baby that will always bind us together." Her hand dropped to her stomach, while she held Heath's bitter black gaze.

"Roland's baby—a Saxon baby." There was weary acceptance in his words.

"No! Not Roland's baby. Your baby."

Amy waited with baited breath.

"My baby?" His eyes still flat, revealing none of the burst of emotion she'd expected. "Why are you telling me this now?"

Did Heath think she was lying? She tried to read his inscrutable gaze, and failed. Surely he couldn't think that. Except for leading him to believe the baby was Roland's by changing the length of her pregnancy, she could never remember consciously deceiving anyone in her life.

"Early Christmas present?" She hid her fear beneath a veneer of flippancy. Then instantly regretted it when his eyes lit up—and not with the love she'd deluded herself that she'd glimpsed previously. "Wait. That came out badly. I'm sorry."

The flare of hot anger subsided. He drew a deep breath. "What made you decide that the baby wasn't Roland's?"

What to say now? She couldn't tell him that she'd always known. She felt ashamed at the idea that he'd know she lied. This was so tough. If only he'd soften a little…

But he didn't.

His gaze bored into her until she felt like a bug on a pin. Amy began to fidget. She hated that feeling, as someone who had striven to be good for most of her life, she wasn't accustomed to it. "Quit staring at me like that."

"Or did Dr. Shortt make an error?"

She couldn't let the doctor take the blame. "It was me—and it wasn't a mistake."

His gaze narrowed to black cracks. "It wasn't a mistake?"

"Okay, I lied," Amy confessed baldly, and stared back at him.

Heath blinked. Whatever he'd expected her to say, clearly it hadn't been that. *"You lied?"*

He sounded thrown.

"Yes, I lied. Me, little Miss Goody-Two-Shoes." Her self-mockery hurt.

"I never referred to you as that when you were young."

"Then you must've been the only one." She sighed.

A gleam flashed in the depths of his eyes. "But then perhaps I saw a side of you that no one else ever did. I saw fire."

Horrors. Had he suspected the passion she hadn't even known lurked inside her? She threw him a wary glance. "Fire? That sounds dangerous. I think I prefer to be thought of as boring."

"Goody-Two-Shoes didn't mean everyone thought you were boring. People liked you, Amy. They considered you to be a good example to others. You were kind. Always helpful. Always trustworthy," he finished.

"Sounds boring to me."

He inspected her. "It's those characteristics that have always made you so special."

She swallowed and wished that she'd never lied to him. Even by omission.

"So if I lie, I suppose that means I'm no longer special?"

An emotion she couldn't identify flared in his eyes, then just as quickly it was gone.

"You're still special." It was so soft that she had to strain her ears to hear. "But this changes things."

"How?" she demanded, suddenly very scared.

He shook his head. "I don't know…but believe me, it does. I need to think about it." He rose to his feet.

"You're going out?"

"I need to clear my head. I need to walk."

Amy watched helplessly as the man she'd married, the man she'd known most of her life but only just started to value, walked out on her.

A sick feeling heaved her stomach that had nothing to do with salmonella. She hoped frantically that he would come back. She'd waited too long to tell him the truth...

A hard walk through vineyards and a hike up The Divide failed to ease the turmoil that raged within Heath.

Amy had lied to him.

Three hours after he'd set out, Heath decided only alcohol would cauterise the pain that seared his innards.

Jock, the whiskered barman at the Roaring Boar, welcomed Heath like a prodigal son. "Long time no see."

A glance around revealed that the pub was as popular as ever on Friday nights. "Good to know you're still here, Jock." Heath clapped the barman on the shoulder. Jock had witnessed much of his youthful stupidity and had never said a word.

That's probably what had drawn him back to the Roaring Boar all these years later.

"Aye, I'll be here till the day I die." Jock gave him a wide grin. It faded with his next words. "Terribly sorry to hear about your brother."

"Thanks." Heath hadn't come to talk—or to reminisce. He'd come to get quietly, seriously rip-roaring drunk. "Double bourbon, please."

Jock shot him a hooded look, but held his tongue as he turned to the glass shelving filled with bottles of all shapes and colours behind him.

Heath found a lone seat at the end of the crowded bar counter and wedged himself in between a giant of a man and the panelled wall of the pub. Seconds later a glass landed in front of him with a thud.

Heath picked it up. The glass felt curiously cold and smooth between his fingers, and the amber colour of the bourbon reminded him of Amy's eyes.

Damn, he couldn't even escape her here. Better he moon

over her like a lovesick puppy in the safety of the Roaring Boar rather than in his home.

Her home.

Chosen Valley was *her* home. She belonged there. He couldn't go back. Not until he'd decided what to do.

The baby was his.

Heath still couldn't absorb it. The revelation had shaken him to the soul. Not Roland's child. But his.

The night he'd spent with Amy—the worst and best night of his life—had resulted in a new life.

He raked a shaky hand through his hair and with the other hand raised the glass. The strong smoky smell of the bourbon filled his nostrils.

Heath set the glass down, undrunk.

Amy had known he was the father of her baby. She'd confessed that she'd lied about the dates. Miss Goody-Two-Shoes had lied to him. She'd known the baby had been conceived the night they spent together.

An unwelcome thought struck him. That's why she'd been so devastated at finding out she was pregnant. Roland's reckless, wild younger brother was the last guy she would've picked to father her child. So why the hell had she agreed to marry him?

It certainly wasn't to give Roland's child a chance at a Saxon life.

The answer came in a blinding flash. In Amy's world, marrying her baby's father would be the only thing to do. *The right thing.* He pushed the bourbon away, repelled by the uncompromising odour of raw alcohol and sank his head in his hands. Somehow, there was a profound difference in knowing that she married him because the child was his—not his brother's.

It took away her element of choice.

"No, no, I ha—want to marry you."

Her panicked statement the day in the aquarium came back to haunt him. *I have to marry you.* In her own mind Amy would've had no choice but to marry him. He shut his eyes.

She'd never loved him. Hell, he'd done his best over the past weeks to court her and she was still no closer to falling for him. He opened his eyes and stared blindly at the scarred wooden counter in front of him. Sure, Amy wanted him. But she resented the molten desire that bonded them together.

Groping for the glass, Heath slugged the bourbon back. The heat of the fiery liquor tasted sour in his mouth and he fought the urge to spit it out.

The guy beside him chose that moment to shift his large mass on his stool and jogged his elbow, knocking the rest of the bourbon over Heath. Accepting the man's embarrassed apologies, Heath resisted the urge to swear.

What the hell was he doing here? He had a wife at home. A wife who was pregnant, who'd been ill. A wife who believed he was out taking a walk. He was behaving with the wild, reckless irresponsibility she'd previously accused him of. Getting drunk tonight wasn't going to convince Amy to fall in love with him.

A night spent drinking would only give him a devastating hangover that he didn't need this close to Christmas.

At least Amy no longer believed he loved her. He could've wrung his sister's neck when he'd heard what Megan had revealed to Amy.

Pride and fury had given him no choice but to dissemble when Amy had put him in a corner by questioning whether he loved her.

A man deserved his pride. He wouldn't have Amy pity him. Right now his damned pride was pretty much all he had.

And Amy.

And the baby.

Heath straightened. That was a helluva lot more than he'd

had only a few months ago. Resolution filled him. Despite Amy's lie, his marriage wasn't over. Fate had dealt him a lucky card. He—not his brother—had fathered Amy's baby.

Rising to his feet, Heath dropped a twenty dollar bill on the counter before heading for the door with newfound optimism.

He loved Amy. This baby was his. And he was not going to walk away from that responsibility. Amy would learn that he intended to be beside her for every minute of his child's life.

A walk?

Heath had gone for a walk? Amy paced up and down the living room. A walk that lasted for over five hours? She stopped and peered out the window. It was pitch dark outside.

She had expected him back within an hour. At first she'd practiced what she'd been going to say to apologise for not telling him sooner about the baby. Then she'd grown mad that he'd taken so long. Finally she'd grown worried.

He hadn't answered his cell phone. He hadn't gone to Saxon's Folly. No one there knew where he was.

And that's when she'd grown more mad than before. *Where was he?* The Lamborghini was missing from the four-car garage.

What if…

No, she wasn't letting her mind go down that terror track. She padded back to the hall table and picked up the phone and hit the redial button. It rang and rang. Just as she was about to give up, Heath answered.

She'd never felt so relieved to hear his voice. Hunching her shoulders, she demanded, "Why didn't you answer your phone?"

"I left it in the Lamborghini."

"Where are you?"

There was a burst of static. "I'm just leaving The Roaring Boar."

"The Roaring Boar?" Amy discovered she was crying. "I thought you'd been in an accident, that you might be dead. But you're only drunk!"

"Amy?"

He shouldn't be driving. She was so angry that she couldn't speak. *How dare he do this to her?*

"Amy? Are you there? Are you okay?"

No, she wasn't okay. She was furious. She was terrified. "Yes," she mumbled. "I'm okay."

"I'm not drunk." His voice grew clearer as the reception improved. "I didn't even finish the one drink I ordered. But if you had to smell me now, you wouldn't believe that."

She fished in the pocket of her dressing gown for a tissue. "Why?"

"Someone spilt bourbon over me. My drink."

Good grief. "Did you get into a fight?" That would be typical of Heath–the–hell-raiser. And far worse than getting drunk...or reeking of alcohol.

"No fight. Nothing happened." Another burst of static. "...home."

"What did you say?"

"I'm coming home."

The line went dead.

Heath was coming home. Amy liked the sound of that. She liked it very much. The misery of the past hours drained away, replaced by a blossom of hope. She wiped the tearstains from her face with the crumpled tissue and considered why those few words—*I'm coming home*—had brought the comfort that she'd desperately needed.

Her hand rested on her stomach as she made her way back to the living room and dropped down onto the sofa to await Heath's arrival. She could've sworn she felt a tiny flutter as she finally made sense of why she'd been so upset by Heath's extended absence.

Amy's breath caught in her throat as the knowledge sank in. She'd been so worried—not just because she feared for his safety. It was more than that. Much more...

She'd fallen in love with Heath Saxon.

Twelve

Heath strode into the house and dropped his keys on the intricately carved chest in the hall. The heavy wooden front door thudded shut behind him. The fresh clean scent of lemon and beeswax lingered, overlaid by a hint of tuberose. Quickening his step, he made for the living room.

It was empty.

Not even the flickering of the Christmas lights on the tree could fill the void that opened inside him.

Of course Amy hadn't waited up for him. Why should she?

She'd told him that the baby she carried was his. He'd been so shaken he'd told her he needed time—a walk to clear his thoughts.

How had his desertion made her feel? He remembered how horrified she'd been to discover she was pregnant. No wonder. The wrong Saxon brother had fathered her child.

Then a memory of the hesitant, hopeful expression in her eyes when she'd told him flashed through his head. And the despair that had followed when he'd said he needed to think, that he was going for a walk.

He gave a groan.

Had Amy imagined he was leaving?

Because he had walked away from her—and he hadn't come home. No, instead he'd gone to the Roaring Boar. Now he stank of bourbon.

Selfish!

Heath gave a groan of self-disgust, his nose wrinkling in distaste at the alcoholic odour that clung to him.

He needed a shower. Then he needed to apologize to Amy. For not listening when she'd needed him to hear her explanation. For walking away. For causing her to worry. And perhaps once he'd apologized, he'd be able to salvage something from the mess he'd made of everything tonight.

Because Amy and the baby meant the world to him.

Swiveling on his heel, Heath exited the living room and headed upstairs. But when he entered the master bedroom, he came to an abrupt halt. Amy wasn't there. Yet the bedside lamps had been switched on, and they cast a gold glow over the rich colours of the bed cover. Amy's dressing gown lay slung over the end of the bed, and her distinctive tuberose fragrance hung in the air.

A noise from the adjoining en suite attracted his attention. His heart quickening, Heath made for the bathroom.

Amy stared at her reflection in the wide mirror. The discovery that she loved Heath had shaken her. She thought about the surprise and joy that had filled her when Megan had said Heath loved her. Why hadn't she put two and two together and realized what he meant to her then?

If only Heath actually loved her in return....

Heath wanted her, that much she knew. She scanned her features in the mirror. Despite her recent illness, her skin glowed. Pregnancy suited her. Maybe they could build on the attraction that sizzled between them...and on the protectiveness and tenderness he displayed toward her. Maybe Heath could grow to love her.

She slid her hands over the silken nightdress, measuring the changes in her body—her full breasts, the curve of her stomach. Heath's baby had made her beautiful.

A sound behind her caused her to turn her head. She met Heath's hooded gaze.

"You're back," she said after a charged moment, hastily dropping her hands from her body.

Heath moved forward with swift grace. "I'm sorry I caused you to worry."

His gaze held hers and she read the sincerity there. "I thought..." Her voice trailed away.

"I know what you imagined." There was an intensity in his eyes that caused her pulse to quicken. "I should've realized you would worry I'd crashed the Lamborghini when I didn't come home. I have no excuse."

"Apology accepted." She owed him a much bigger apology for her behavior—for her failure to tell him the truth. Her gaze fell beneath his piercing regard. Only then did she notice the stains on his shirt. She inhaled deeply.

"Yes, I smell like a bar. I need a shower," he said and reached to turn the faucet on.

The sound of rushing water broke the sudden silence that stretched between them.

Heath turned his head, his eyes blazing with emotion. "Amy, I'm so glad that our baby is okay."

Our baby.

Hot emotion balled into a tight knot above her heart. Her throat tight, she murmured, "Me, too."

Heath stripped off the bourbon-soaked shirt and dropped it on the marble floor, revealing his gloriously muscled torso. The rest of this clothes followed as he shed them in economic movements.

Amy found she could no longer breathe.

Heath quirked an eyebrow. "Coming?"

Amy blinked to snap herself out of the thrall that held her. Slowly she shed her night dress, and by the time she stepped into the shower cubicle it was hot and steamy.

Heath's hands, slick with soap, closed on her upper arms. He stroked her flesh with long, smooth movements.

"So beautiful," he whispered.

Her nipples pebbled under his touch and pleasurable sensations rippled through her as his strong hands massaged her and the hot water sluiced over her.

Too soon he ushered her out the shower and wrapped her in a thick white bath sheet before swinging her in his arms.

"Heath, you don't need to carry me."

He shot her a grin. "I enjoy it, indulge me. You're such a little thing."

She froze as he set her down beside the vast bed and rubbed her dry. Little thing? "I never realised. I'm a petite brunette."

"You forgot pretty."

She flushed. "So by marrying me you're acting true to type."

"Amy-love, you're the pretty, petite brunette prototype."

"What do you mean?" The breathlessness was back.

But he stood in front of her, nude and magnificent. "We're talking too much." Then he was kissing her and her mind cleared of all thought. All she could do was feel.

He stripped the bath sheet away and tumbled her naked onto the bed before following her down.

His hands touched her belly, his palms moulding the gentle rise where the baby was starting to make its presence known.

"This is more than I ever hoped for." Heath kissed the soft skin of her stomach, and Amy dug her fingers into the corded muscles in his upper arms.

"What do you mean?"

"You…" another kiss and then he raised his head "…and our baby."

"You hoped?" She groped for the words.

"Oh, yes, I hoped. And prayed. Every day of my life. But I never believed it would happen."

"You mean us?"

He didn't answer. Instead, he ran his hands over her thighs, parted them and traced the intricate folds between her legs.

Amy gasped.

His head dipped to follow where his fingers had touched and in the minutes that followed Amy's breath grew ragged.

Finally she pushed him away. "My turn."

He resisted for a moment. But she wouldn't allow him to stop her. When her mouth closed over him, he shuddered, every muscle in his lean frame taut.

She licked and sucked at his hard flesh with an avid curiosity that almost drove him mad. Once. Twice. He fought to stop himself from coming in hot tangy blasts.

When he could take no more, he groaned and flipped her on her back. He planted a gentle kiss on her pouting lips and slowly, his weight propped on his arms, he sank into her.

With slow deliberate strokes he drove the ever-increasing spirals of pleasure higher and higher. Watching her, he waited until the moment that her lashes fluttered over those incredible, glowing eyes.

One more slow thrust and they both came apart.

Afterwards, Heath reclined back against stuffed continental pillows and held his wife in his arms. For a long time they both lay quietly under the covers. Finally, he turned his head and met her sated gaze. "There's something you need to know."

She tensed and her eyes grew wary. "What?"

"That I'm never going to walk away from my child." He slipped a hand under the cover and rested it on her stomach.

"Or you. This marriage truly is for better or worse, even though I rewrote our wedding vows."

She didn't speak, simply held his gaze.

He didn't like the silence. He found he wanted to know what she was thinking. So he lifted his hand from her belly and brought it out to brush her hair behind her ears, then asked, "How could you be so certain that the baby was mine?"

The smile that she gave him was bittersweet. "That's easy. I never made love with Roland."

Shock slammed through him. "What?"

"There was only ever you."

"Only me? But why?"

Curled into him, Amy watched as the glazed expression in the ebony eyes slowly cleared. "Because I wanted a white wedding night."

"Why didn't you tell me…stop me?" Horror filled his face. "I would've stopped. Even though it would probably have killed me, I would never have taken that precious gift from you if I'd known."

"What was the point?" She shrugged and her bare skin rubbed against him, arousing frissons of awareness. "I'd guarded my virginity…it caused terrible grief between me and Roland…and then he died. It hardly seemed worth prizing any longer."

Heath swallowed, his Adam's apple moving. "I appreciate that. Thank you for telling me."

"Okay, my turn to ask a question." Amy glanced up at him through her lashes. "What did you mean I was the prototype?"

Heath grinned at her. "I knew you'd ask that. You're the love of my life. The woman I searched for in every other female I dated. The woman I believed would never be mine."

"You're joking? Since when?" Amy pulled away from him, her eyes wide with disbelief. Then, more subdued as she took in the pain behind his grin, she said, "You're not joking. You're serious."

He pulled her back to where she'd rested before she'd drawn away. "Since you were sixteen." His mouth slanted. "I thought you were too young. I intended to wait for you."

Amy covered her mouth with her hands. "And I fell for Roland. Told the whole world on my seventeenth birthday— after he gave me the gorgeous locket that convinced me he was my soul mate. Stupid child."

Heath's eyes dimmed for an instant. She got the impression he was hesitating, then he said, "I told myself all I wanted was for you to be happy. I lied. I wanted you for myself."

"Oh, Heath. And Roland and I were going to get married."

"That's one of the reasons I made myself so scarce. My fight with Dad wasn't the only reason I stayed away from Saxon's Folly, except for the odd dinner. I didn't want to hear about the wedding arrangements. I'm a sinner, sweet innocent Amy. Every wicked thing you've ever heard about me is true."

"You won't scare me, Heath." She planted a kiss on the side of his neck.

He suppressed the urge to grab her and haul her beneath him, and start loving her all over again. "I should," he growled.

She lifted her head and gave him an indecipherable look. "You couldn't have done anything worse than what I've done."

"You?" Heath shook his head in denial. Not Amy. "You're as near to perfect as it gets."

"I'm not. I'm—" she broke off, averting her face. Then she said, "So what have you done that's so terrible?"

"I coveted my brother's fiancée!"

Her breath caught with an audible gasp. "Heath—"

"And then I—"

"Stop. You tried to warn me that Roland wouldn't suit me…"

"That wasn't wholly self-motivated. He'd always had girl-friends you never knew about. I was worried about you."

"But no one ever told me."

"I couldn't. Roland was my brother. I owed him some

loyalty. And I was in the worse position. If I told you…and it came out how I felt about you, I'd look like the world's most dishonourable jerk."

Amy wriggled along his body until she rested as close as she could get. Gazing into his eyes she said, "I can understand that. So you tried to warn me off. But I refused to listen. Until that final night. I broke up with Roland—did you know that?"

Heath shook his head.

"I'd heard he was having an affair. I confronted him. I told him that I wanted fidelity from the man I married…that I didn't want someone who cheated on me." She glanced away from his perceptive eyes for a brief moment. "That's why I felt so guilty when he died. I'd promised to marry him and I broke that promise. If we hadn't fought, he might not have died."

"Oh, Amy!" Heath gathered her close. "Never feel guilty. He breached the promise of trust and fidelity first. You had every reason to end your engagement."

"He didn't want to break up. He was upset. Much more upset than I expected." She hauled in a deep breath. This was so hard. Living with it had made her miserable for months. "But I insisted. It was my fault. I caused the accident. I broke his concentration."

"You can't blame yourself. You didn't want Roland dead. Nor did I." He sighed. "I loved my brother." He cupped her cheek with his calloused fingers. "And I loved you. It was a hell of a place to be in."

"You know what I don't get?" Amy paused. "Why did Roland want to marry me if he couldn't give up other women?"

"Who knows? Maybe he loved you as much as I did, despite the other women." Then Heath snapped his fingers. "He knew about your virginity pledge?"

"Oh, yes."

"Perhaps that was it. Roland always loved a challenge."

Amy considered that. "It's possible, although we'll never know."

"What's important is not to forget the parts of Roland that we all loved. His energy. His generosity. His enthusiasm." Heath's eyes were gentle. "And always remember that I love you."

"Oh, Heath, I love you, too. I'm so lucky to have found you."

He grinned, a happy carefree grin. "Amy-love, you had to look a long way to find me next door in the house where you grew up."

"Let's just say I missed the obvious. But now that I've found you, that's it."

"I'm not going anywhere. I chose you a long time ago."

He pulled her toward him and kissed her gently, and Amy knew that was a promise he would never break.

Christmas Eve, the day of the Saxon's Folly Summer Festival, dawned fresh and bright. By midafternoon the rhythmic sound of jazz music echoed through the vineyard and over the surrounding hills.

People streamed through the curved gates and by three o'clock the grassy expanse around the bandstand was covered with picnic blankets as couples and families ate and listened to the melodic strains as one band followed another.

"Would you like some cotton candy?" Heath asked Amy as they walked past a row of food stalls which had been set up for today's event.

She eyed the pink candy. "I think I'll pass until I've had some real food. And then we have to find the family."

All the Saxons were here today. And Amy's father, too. Earlier in the week, Joshua and Alyssa had been away in Auckland, necessitating a delay in telling the family the truth about the baby's parentage. But they could delay no longer.

"We'll round everyone up." Heath scanned the swelling

crowd. "Though I'm starting to have my doubts about getting everyone together at the same time. It's a madhouse today."

A few stalls along, Heath bought a platter of hot fresh rolls and roasted vegetables, and they returned to where he'd set up chairs under a large oak tree on the perimeter of the grassy clearing. The vegetables tasted sweet and the bread was crusty on the outside and soft when she broke it open.

"Feeling okay?" he asked.

"Completely." She drew a deep breath. "Thank you for looking after me for all those days that I was ill."

"In sickness and in health," he said, his eyes intense.

"We didn't say that. You changed the vows, remember?"

"But those go without saying…and to love." His eyes glowed, and warmth suffused her.

Before Amy could respond, a burst of laughter broke the mood between them.

"Heath Saxon?"

The woman who stood beside the picnic blanket was confidently stunning, her face known in every home throughout New Zealand. Kelly Christie. Uncertainty pierced Amy. Had the beautiful Kelly been one of Heath's conquests? For a brief instant, every fear that Amy had ever had about falling for Heath returned. Then she shoved the crazy doubts away.

Heath had married her.

He loved her. Only her.

Her nerves steadied. Heath had never done anything to make her doubt him. He'd been steadfast and caring. How could she doubt him now? The tall, leggy blonde television goddess wasn't even his usual type. No pretty, petite brunette. Amy started to smile as the momentary doubt and uncertainty evaporated.

"It's wonderful to meet you, Heath," Kelly simpered. "If you don't mind, I'll bring the cameras over and film you for a little while and then I'd like to ask you a few questions for our midday Christmas show tomorrow."

Heath revealed no pleasure at the prospect of cozying up with the TV hostess for millions to see. Kelly wasn't an ex, Amy realized. And judging from his frown, Kelly had failed to impress.

Already Heath was shaking his head. "Not today, Kelly. It's been a busy week. My wife and I are taking private time out to enjoy the concert."

"Of course, your wife. Emily, isn't it?"

"Amy," she corrected. All animation vanished from the blonde's features and her pale blue eyes turned to slowly inspect Amy.

This woman hated her.

Why?

Amy didn't even know her, could've sworn she'd never met Kelly. Instinctively, Amy shifted closer to Heath to escape the venom.

His arm came around her, warm and solid. Kelly didn't miss the gesture. She laughed. "So how does it feel to be the fortunate woman to have snared two of the gorgeous Saxon men, Amy?"

Then Amy knew.

This woman had been Roland's lover, the celebrity she'd heard rumours of and confronted him about. Had his mistress loved Roland? The hurt lurking below the rage in those azure eyes suggested that she had.

Amy looked at her with pity.

Kelly had beauty, a fabulous career, but she'd fallen for another woman's man. A man engaged to be married who showed no sign of abandoning his hometown fiancée.

How that must've stung.

Roland had cheated both of them. By a tragic turn of fate, Amy had escaped marrying him. She'd married Heath instead. Tender. Protective. Fiercely loyal. A man worthy of her love.

She could afford to be generous.

"Kelly, if you call after Christmas, perhaps we can set up a time for you to interview the Saxon family as we look forward to the next harvest." Amy gave the other woman her sweetest smile. "You and your cameramen would get access to the wineries on both sides of The Divide, Saxon's Folly and Chosen Valley. An exclusive, if you like."

Kelly looked startled. Then her composure returned and she gave Amy a suspicious narrow-eyed look.

Amy held her gaze, refusing to be intimidated.

Finally, Kelly smiled, a genuine smile that glowed with charisma and revealed not an iota of resentment. "I'd like that very much, Amy Saxon. Thank you."

She turned to go.

Amy sneaked a glance at Heath. His eyes glittered a warning at the TV hostess. Dangerous. Confidently, Amy linked her fingers through his.

"Kelly," she called.

The TV hostess swiveled on her white high heels.

"Feel free to announce that Heath and I are expecting a baby on your Christmas day exclusive." The woman's eyes widened in stunned amazement. "The first Saxon grandchild," Amy added. "And you're the first to know. Please give us a chance to tell the family—so keep it confidential until your show at noon tomorrow."

Kelly shook her head, her eyes disbelieving. "You don't mind?"

Amy turned her head and met Heath's incredulous gaze. "Everyone's going to find out sometime," she told him. "Kelly might as well get the first break on the news."

"Amy, it's not hard to see why the Saxon men adore you. Thanks again." And with a wave and a flash of that famous white smile, she was gone.

"I'm not sure that was a good idea." Heath's hand tightened around her fingers. "I may get Alyssa to contact Kelly's station to cancel that interview."

"I should have checked with you first." Amy's heart dropped. "I thought the publicity might be good for both wineries—her show is very popular." And how could she explain that her heart had ached for Kelly?

"Kelly Christie can cause a lot of trouble."

He wasn't annoyed with her. He was concerned for her. This was Heath in protector mode. The certainty solidified. She squeezed his fingers. "If you're referring to her affair with Roland, then I have to say I think you're wrong."

"You know about that?"

For the second time in minutes, Amy saw that she'd shocked him.

"I told you I knew Roland was having an affair shortly before he died. Until just now I didn't know the identity of the woman."

"But Kelly didn't say anything—"

"She didn't have to. I knew. She was jealous…and upset. The pain and unhappiness were in her eyes."

Heath fell silent. Tugging her hand, he pulled her close and said, "That was an incredibly classy—and gutsy— thing to do." Heath nuzzled her hair. "I think you have a fan for life."

"I'm sure she won't step out of line."

"She won't get the chance," Heath said darkly. "No one will harm you while I have breath in my body."

Amy basked in the glow of Heath's possessive words as dusk fell and the stage lights came on, suffusing the estate with a glow.

Heath's brother, Joshua and Alyssa joined them and a little later Megan made her way over, too.

"Where are the parents?" asked Heath.

"They left," said Megan. "Mom said they had some serious stuff to discuss. But they were holding hands."

"Dad has a lot to make up for," Joshua said. "But I hope that Mother forgives him."

Heath and Amy exchanged glances. Their news would have to wait another day.

"It's been a wonderful day," said Amy dreamily.

"Now the work starts on next year's festival."

Alyssa rolled her eyes at Joshua's droll observation.

"Hey, don't look like that," her fiancé said, "I know you loved every moment of it."

"Actually, I did," said Alyssa. "I love being part of the Saxon family."

Joshua leant over and gave his fiancée a lingering kiss. "I'm so glad I found you."

Pleasure spread through Amy at their clear love for each other. Absently, she touched the locket around her neck. She'd have to get a picture of Heath to put in there. She'd removed the image of Roland the night before the wedding. It had been the right thing to do. But Heath was her love now. She wanted his image close to her breast.

"That's a lovely piece of jewellery," Alyssa said, leaning forward to get a closer look. "Victorian, is it?"

Amy nodded.

"Roland bought you that for your birthday," Joshua recalled. "I remember. Was it your eighteenth birthday? He dragged us all along to help him shop for your present, do you remember?"

"It was Amy's seventeenth. He wanted my opinion because I was a girl." Megan was laughing.

Amy's fingers stilled. All these years she'd cherished the locket, believing Roland had chosen it for her. "You mean you chose it?" she asked Megan.

Megan shook her head. "Not me. Heath did. I would've

gone for something art deco–inspired. Heath pointed out that you loved lace and old-fashioned fripperies. He found the Victorian heart. He wanted to buy it for you, but Roland paid for it before he could. I think Heath sent you flowers instead."

"Yes, he did." She'd almost forgotten about the lovely bunch of long-stemmed white roses.

"So if I'd given you a romantic Victorian locket studded with diamonds, would you have decided I was the one?"

Amy's eyes met her husband's as she remembered his words. He'd known. And she hadn't.

"Didn't you know, Amy?"

Megan's uncanny question brought her back to the present. "No, Heath never breathed a word."

"Oh, dear!" Megan covered her mouth with her hand. "Have I put my foot in it again?"

"Looks like it." Joshua unfolded himself from where he was sitting. "Should we go dance, darling?" he asked Alyssa.

"I think I'd better go, too." Megan weaved her way into the crowd.

Amy didn't look away from Heath. There was nothing she needed to say. He must've read it in her eyes.

"Roland was wrong for you."

"I was so young." Too young."

"He should've known better." Heath's eyes were steadfast. "He was my brother, I loved him. But he wasn't capable of committing to one woman."

"You love me." It was a statement, not a question.

"Always and forever." His intensity was palpable.

"I must be the luckiest woman in the world." Amy fell silent when a group of children dressed as angels wearing long white robes with big silver wings and holding candles filed past. At the base of the rotunda, they formed a circle. The band burst into a funky version of "Joy to the World" and the dancing crowd swayed and sang along.

"I hope there are angels where Roland is now."

Heath chuckled. "If there are, I'm sure Roland will find them."

Amy shook her head even as she laughed. "I suppose you're right."

"Tired?" asked Heath.

"There are still two bands to play," she said.

"I know. But I thought you might have had enough."

She caught the concern for her in his eyes. Something softened, and heat flared inside her. "Perhaps it's time to find a different party."

The skin across his cheeks grew taut. Amy could feel tension winding through his every muscle.

"What are we waiting for?"

Epilogue

The Christmas bells sounded joyous to Amy as she and Heath exited the stone church hand in hand after the early morning sermon.

The sun had already risen over the sea and the sky was suffused with shades of pink and orange, and a golden glow heralded her and Heath's first Christmas together.

Amy glanced sideways at her husband. "Thank you for coming with me this morning."

His hand tightened around hers and she knew without words that the service had moved him as much as it had her. The message of love that the priest had delivered had been so right for her and Heath, it had brought tears to her eyes. And it made her feel closer to the man beside her. Amy was no longer afraid that she'd failed to live up to her good girl reputation. More importantly, she'd found love. Real love. Heath was her match, her mate, her equal.

She'd said a silent prayer for Roland, too, resting his memory in peace. She suspected Heath had, too.

Her husband held the passenger door of the Lamborghini open and she ducked in. Within minutes they were roaring down the long, tree-lined drive of Saxon's Folly.

The house came into sight, a white Victorian homestead tucked in against the hill covered with rows of vines. The great wooden front doors were already open.

Their arms filled with gaily wrapped gifts, Heath and Amy found the family in the sitting room and added their offerings to the enormous heap of wrapped gifts under the evergreen tree.

Across the room, Ralph Wright rose to his feet and gave Amy a kiss on the cheek before shaking Heath's hand. "Merry Christmas to you both."

"Oh, it is." Amy smiled at her father.

Megan shut the cell phone she'd been texting on and came over to give them both an enthusiastic hug. Alyssa and Joshua were more circumspect, but Amy could feel their love and affection.

"Heath, dear," said Kay Saxon, "Rafaelo and Caitlyn just called to wish us a Merry Christmas—they send their love. Rafaelo says we must all go visit. Maybe we should consider visiting next Christmas."

"There will be their wedding too," pointed out Alyssa. "Speaking of which, Joshua and I have finally set a date: Valentine's Day falls on a Saturday next year. So make sure you note that down."

Kay perched herself on the arm of the leather chair where her husband sat and gave him a loving smile. Returning the smile, Phillip put an arm around Kay's waist, and his face softened with love.

Amy exchanged a pleased glance with Heath. It looked like

the rift between his parents had been mended. From the corner of her eye, Amy saw that Alyssa had noticed it, too, and was whispering something in Joshua's ear.

Heath led Amy over to his parents. "Mom, Dad, we've got a gift for you." He looked across to Amy's father. "And you, too, Ralph."

Kay and Phillip broke out of their self-absorption and looked at them with interest. Ralph came closer.

"You've decided to stay at Saxon's Folly, I hope?" said Phillip.

Heath nodded. "Yes, I'd like that, Dad. But that's not the gift we came to tell you about." Heath drew Amy closer. "We want your blessing."

"For your gift?" Phillip frowned.

Kay looked puzzled. "Our blessing?"

"I'm the father of Amy's baby," Heath announced into the waiting silence. "Our baby will be due in June."

"I'm not surprised," said Ralph.

Then everyone started to talk at once. There was laughter and tears and hugs and when it had all settled back to normal, Heath grinned at Amy and mouthed, "I love you."

With a soft smile she responded by tugging his hand and kissing him sedately under a sprig of mistletoe.

At last the family all made their way to the Christmas tree where the gifts awaited.

"Next Christmas there'll be a new member to add to the family circle." Heath smiled down at Amy and she knew that he was thinking that their marriage, their child, had hastened the healing in the family. "The first grandchild."

"The first of many from the Saxon brides," concluded Kay as she handed a wrapped gift to Megan. "Be happy, all of you. Love each other every day of your lives."

Her eyes glowing with joy, Amy looked around the circle

of familiar faces. "It's wonderful to have a family Christmas together."

And everyone heartily agreed.

* * * * *

One

Hunter Cabot, Navy SEAL, had a healing bullet wound in his side, thirty days' leave and, apparently, a wife he'd never met.

On the drive into his hometown of Springville, California, he stopped for gas at Charlie Evans's service station. That's where the trouble started.

"Hunter! Man, it's good to see you! Margie didn't tell us you were coming home."

"Margie?" Hunter leaned back against the front fender of his black pickup truck and winced as his side gave a small twinge of pain. Silently then, he watched as the man he'd known since high school filled his tank.

Charlie grinned, shook his head and pumped gas. "Guess your wife was lookin' for a little 'alone' time with you, huh?"

"My—" Hunter couldn't even say the word. *Wife?* He didn't have a wife. "Look, Charlie..."

"Don't blame her, of course," his friend said with a wink as he finished up and put the gas cap back on. "You being gone all the time with the SEALs must be hard on the ol' love life."

He'd never had any complaints, Hunter thought, frowning at the man still talking a mile a minute. "What're you—"

"Bet Margie's anxious to see you. She told us all about that R and R trip you two took to Bali." Charlie's dark brown eyebrows lifted and wiggled.

"Charlie..."

"Hey, it's okay, you don't have to say a thing, man."

What the hell could he say? Hunter shook his head, paid for his gas and as he left, told himself Charlie was just losing it. Maybe the guy had been smelling gas fumes too long.

But as it turned out, it wasn't just Charlie. Stopped at a red light on Main Street, Hunter glanced out his window to smile at Mrs. Harker, his second-grade teacher who was now at least a hundred years old. In the middle of the crosswalk, the old lady stopped and shouted, "Hunter Cabot, you've got yourself a wonderful wife. I hope you appreciate her."

Scowling now, he only nodded at the old woman—the only teacher who'd ever scared the crap out of him. What the hell was going on here? Was everyone but him nuts?

His temper beginning to boil, he put up with a few more comments about his "wife" on the drive through town before finally pulling into the wide, circular drive leading to the Cabot mansion. Hunter didn't have a clue what was going on, but he planned to get to the bottom of it. Fast.

He grabbed his duffel bag, stalked into the house and paid no attention to the housekeeper, who ran at him, fluttering both hands. "Mr. Hunter!"

"Sorry, Sophie," he called out over his shoulder as he took the stairs two at a time. "Need a shower, then we'll talk."

He marched down the long, carpeted hallway to the rooms that were always kept ready for him. In his suite, Hunter tossed the duffel down and stopped dead. The shower in his bathroom was running. His *wife?*

Anger and curiosity boiled in his gut, creating a churning mass that had him moving forward without even thinking about it. He opened the bathroom door to a wall of steam and the sound of a woman singing—off-key. Margie, no doubt.

Well, if she was his wife...Hunter walked across the room, yanked the shower door open and stared in at a curvy, naked, temptingly wet woman.

She whirled to face him, slapping her arms across her naked body while she gave a short, terrified scream.

Hunter smiled. "Hi, honey. I'm home."

* * * * *

Be sure to look for
AN OFFICER AND A MILLIONAIRE
by USA TODAY *bestselling author Maureen Child.*
Available January 2009 from Silhouette Desire.

Silhouette

SPECIAL EDITION™

The Bravos meet the Jones Gang
as two of Christine Rimmer's famous
Special Edition families come together
in one very special book.

THE STRANGER
AND TESSA JONES

by

CHRISTINE RIMMER

Snowed in with an amnesiac stranger during a
freak blizzard, Tessa Jones soon finds out her
guest is none other than heartbreaker Ash Bravo.
And that's when things really heat up....

*Available January 2009
wherever you buy books.*

REQUEST YOUR FREE BOOKS!

2 FREE NOVELS PLUS 2 FREE GIFTS!

Passionate, Powerful, Provocative!

Silhouette®
Romantic
SUSPENSE

Sparked by Danger,
Fueled by Passion.

Justine Davis

Baby's Watch

Former bad boy Ryder Colton has never felt a
connection to much, so he's shocked when he feels
one to the baby he helps deliver, and her mother.
Ana Morales doesn't quite trust this stranger, but
when her daughter is taken by a smuggling ring,
she teams up with him in the hope of rescuing her
baby. With nowhere to turn she has no choice but
to trust Ryder with her life...and her heart.

Available January 2009 wherever books are sold.

Look for the final installment of
the Coltons: Family First miniseries,
A Hero of Her Own by Carla Cassidy in February 2009.

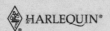

INTRIGUE

Sabrina Hunter works hard as a police detective
and a single mom. She's confronted with her
past when a murder scene draws in both her
and her son's father, Patrick Martinez. But when
a creepy sensation of being watched turns into
deadly threats, she must learn to trust the man
she once loved.

SECRETS IN
FOUR CORNERS

BY

DEBRA WEBB

**Available January 2009
wherever you buy books.**

You're invited to join our Tell Harlequin Reader Panel!

By joining our new reader panel you will:

- Receive Harlequin® books—they are FREE and yours to keep with no obligation to purchase anything!
- Participate in fun online surveys
- Exchange opinions and ideas with women just like you
- Have a say in our new book ideas and help us publish the best in women's fiction

In addition, you will have a chance to win great prizes and receive special gifts! See Web site for details. Some conditions apply. Space is limited.

To join, visit us at
www.TellHarlequin.com.

Silhouette® Desire

COMING NEXT MONTH

SDCNMBPA1208